"What could a sharp-tongued lady barracuda possibly know about passion?" Logan asked, glowering down at Krista. "My guess is, not a thing!"

Suddenly they were standing so close that a sheet of paper couldn't have been slipped between them. "Sure of that, are you?" she said huskily, her voice unsteady.

"What *do* you know?" he asked. His lips moved closer with each softly spoken word. "Show me."

Krista inhaled shakily. "Logan," she said in a voice she hardly recognized as her own. It was full of want and need, yet soft with surrender. She wasn't prepared for the urgency that spun through her, for the wave of desire that sent her reeling. He was going to kiss her, and she wanted him to, far too much. . . .

WHAT ARE *LOVESWEPT* ROMANCES?

They are stories of true romance and touching emotion. We believe those two very important ingredients are constants in our highly sensual and very believable stories in the *LOVESWEPT* line. Our goal is to give you, the reader, stories of consistently high quality that may sometimes make you laugh, sometimes make you cry, but are always fresh and creative and contain many delightful surprises within their pages.

Most romance fans read an enormous number of books. Those they truly love, they keep. Others may be traded with friends and soon forgotten. We hope that each *LOVESWEPT* romance will be a treasure—a "keeper." We will always try to publish

LOVE STORIES YOU'LL NEVER FORGET
BY AUTHORS YOU'LL ALWAYS REMEMBER

The Editors

LOVESWEPT® • 183

Barbara Boswell
Tangles

BANTAM BOOKS
TORONTO • NEW YORK • LONDON • SYDNEY • AUCKLAND

TANGLES

A Bantam Book / March 1987

LOVESWEPT® *and the wave device are registered trademarks of Bantam Books, Inc. Registered in U.S. Patent and Trademark Office and elsewhere.*

If you would be interested in receiving protective vinyl covers for your Loveswept books, please write to this address for information:

> Loveswept
> Bantam Books
> P.O. Box 985
> Hicksville, NY 11802

ISBN 0-553-21811-5

Published simultaneously in the United States and Canada

One

"She's staring at me," Ned Bolger said to his attorney, Krista Conway. His gaze was riveted on the rigid figure of his soon-to-be-ex-wife who was glowering across the courtroom at him. "She's trying to intimidate me! She thinks she can shake me up and make me blow my cool. Look at her!" He grasped the sleeve of his attorney's impeccably tailored heather-blue silk suit jacket. "Make her stop staring at me!"

Krista carefully disentangled his fingers from her sleeve. "Don't pay any attention to her, Ned," she said soothingly. "Don't even glance in her direction if it rattles you. Just try to relax and stay calm."

Which was easier said than done, Krista thought. In a bitterly contested divorce, emotions ran as high as in a murder trial. And the Bolger divorce was one of the most bitterly contested divorces she'd ever handled. From the homicidal glares Ned and Elaine Bolger were throwing at each other, this might well escalate into a murder trial.

Ross Perry, Elaine Bolger's attorney, got up from his table and walked over to Krista. Leaning over, he whispered to her. "Wearing your bulletproof vest?"

She smiled up at him, amused that his thoughts had followed along the same lines as hers.

Both Ned and Elaine Bolger scowled at their attorneys. Obviously, Krista thought, the Bolgers couldn't bear to see their attorneys exchange a civil word, let alone a smile.

"The lovely Elaine looks ready to incinerate you along with Ned and me," Krista said softly to Ross. "What gives?"

Though she and Ross Perry were friendly—the three dozen or so lawyers who practiced exclusively divorce law in Maryland's affluent Montgomery County all dealt amicably with one another—in court they generally remained aloof, sometimes even adversarial, for their embattled clients' sakes. Whatever had prompted Ross to speak to her in this volatile atmosphere must be important enough to risk the wrath of both their clients.

It was. "I just got word," Ross said, "that Judge Benton was hospitalized this morning. His ulcer kicked up again. We've been reassigned to another judge."

Krista's dark blue eyes widened, and she drew in a sharp breath. "I was counting on Benton presiding," she muttered, more to herself than to Perry. She knew Judge Benton well, was familiar with all his foibles and prejudices, and had fitted her case and her client to suit him.

Ross grimaced. "That makes two of us." He'd obviously tailored his case to Judge Benton as well, Krista thought. It would have been an interesting battle.

"Are you ready for the really bad news?" Ross went on. He paused dramatically before dropping his bombshell. "We're getting a visiting judge from Garrett County."

"Garrett County!" Krista echoed with a muffled groan. Garrett County was in the mountains of western Maryland, and the distance between that rural county and Montgomery County, the sophisticated, wealthy enclave bordering the District of Columbia, was far more than geographic.

"Garrett County," repeated Ross. "They drive pickup trucks and wear baseball caps and talk with hillbilly accents out there. Bet they don't much cotton to dee-vorce in those parts, either," he added, lapsing into a dreadful twang. "Shucks, how do you reckon a down-home country judge will take to a bunch of city slickers like you and me and the Bolgers?"

"If he hears any trace of that atrocious hayseed accent, he might find you in contempt of court." Krista tried to sound stern, but her lips quivered into a betraying grin. She happened to catch Elaine Bolger's smoldering stare. "Your client looks ready to explode, Ross. Unless you really are wearing a bulletproof vest, you'd better get over there and calm her down."

Ross gave a brief nod and rejoined the outraged Elaine at their table. He solicitously leaned toward her, smiling his practiced smile and nodding. Krista admired his technique as she watched him smoothly diffuse his client's anger.

Ross Perry was a skilled and highly successful divorce lawyer, right up there in the exclusive barracuda/bomber class with Krista Conway herself. Krista enjoyed crossing swords with him. He was one of the few in the area who was her match. There even had been a case or two in which he'd bested her.

She had to admire him for that because at thirty-three and ten years out of law school, Krista was seldom bested or even equaled in hammering out divorce settlements. Her skill had gained her a fame that made her seem even more invincible and intimidating than she actually was, and Krista knew it. Sometimes it amused her, other times it depressed her. She was fully aware that she was a living, breathing mass of contradictions. A high-stakes divorce lawyer who deeply believed in marriage. A master of legal strategy and tactics who secretly yearned that one day true love would find her.

Her client Ned Bolger, however, knew none of this. He knew only of her reputation as Montgomery County's leading big-money divorce lawyer. He thought it well worth it to pay her an exorbitant retainer to keep his wife from emerging the winner in the struggle over their marital assets. He would never have believed that Krista Conway could be saddened by the shattered dreams that a divorce represented.

At this particular moment, Ned was glaring at Ross Perry and Elaine. "What did Perry say? What's Elaine up to now?" he demanded testily.

Krista leaned toward him with a reassuring smile and calmed him with careful and practiced reassurance.

The bailiff entered the courtroom with the judge to announce, "All rise. Court is now in session. The Honorable Logan H. Moore presiding."

His black robe flowing around him, the Honorable Logan H. Moore proceeded to the bench.

His commanding height registered first with Krista. She stared. Logan Moore must be at least six feet three, perhaps six four. Beneath the stately judge's robes were broad shoulders that could easily have filled a professional football player's jersey. And his hands . . . She stared at his long, lean fingers gripping his gavel as he instructed the court to be seated. He had the biggest hands she'd ever seen. From somewhere deep in the recesses of her memory sprang the old college-girl myth about the size of a man's hands in relation to—

Krista instantly relegated that thought back to the deep, dark recesses from whence it came. This was the first time she'd ever fantasized about a *judge*! Of course, all the judges she knew were years—even decades!—older than Garrett County's Logan Moore.

From the silvery tips spun through his thick dark hair, and from his judicial position, she deduced he must be at least forty. A whole generation removed from the seventyish Judge Benton.

Her gaze flicked to his face and quickly scanned it. His features were too harsh to qualify him as classically handsome, but the sharp blade of a nose, the firm jaw and well-shaped mouth were arresting and compellingly masculine. His ebony eyes were alert and intelligent as he looked around the courtroom.

Then those eyes connected with hers. She held his gaze, waiting for him to look away, but he didn't. Krista was well aware of the psychological implications of body language; she'd carefully studied every aspect that she could use to advantage in the courtroom. And from her reading she knew that eye contact that lasted longer than two seconds took on an altogether different meaning from casual observation.

It could become an aggressive challenge. Whoever looked away first was ceding superiority. Despite her increasing discomfort, Krista was not about to cede superiority to a backcountry judge who was probably unaccustomed to dealing with female attorneys and was seeking to assert his masculine ego.

Their gazes held. Had they been two males, the challenge would be pointing toward possible aggressive action. But Krista Conway was a woman and Logan Moore was a man, and their prolonged eye contact slipped swiftly into the sexual arena.

Krista's lashes fluttered involuntarily. The man's magnetism was too strong, and some primal force within her responded accordingly. Her body tightened. She felt breathless, as if she'd just been punched in the stomach. Then the judge's gaze moved past her.

For a split second Krista remained stock-still and listened to her pulses hammering in her ears. Her whole body seemed to be vibrating. She'd never before reacted so intensly to a man's stare. What on earth had come over her? She glanced at her leather briefcase, her pages of notes, in a terrible confusion. When she dared to glance up again, she found the judge watching her.

Once more their gazes locked. Krista's mouth felt dry. Heat slowly suffused her body. She couldn't seem to look away from him. She couldn't move or think or breathe. His gaze was on her mouth now, and she felt its effect as if he'd physically touched her. Her lips parted, and she drew in her breath sharply.

Ned Bolger's frantic whisper finally catapulted her out of her peculiar sensual trance. "Elaine looks so damn smug! She thinks she's won it already, the witch. I can't wait to see her expression after you've shot her and that damn lawyer of hers down. We're going to annihilate them, aren't we?"

Krista glanced at her client and suppressed a sigh. Sometimes it was difficult to deal with, that terrible hostility between a man and a woman who had once loved and lived together as husband and wife. She did her job well, for she believed that divorce was a sad fact of life and that competent professionals were essential to expedite the dissolution of a dead or decaying marriage. But she didn't relish being used as a weapon of revenge. She didn't want to annihilate Elaine Bolger and Ross Perry. She wanted to win fairly a case she'd spent hours of time and effort on.

"The witch," Ned Bolger growled again, shooting his wife a fierce look. Which was returned in full measure by Elaine.

Ross Perry caught Krista's eye and arched his brows slightly. Krista shrugged almost imperceptibly. The case of *Bolger* v. *Bolger* was ready to begin. . . .

"Objection overruled!" Logan Moore decreed with a pound of his gavel. The noise seemed to echo in his head. His temples were throbbing, and the band of tension gripping the top of his head grew even tighter. He had been a judge in Garrett County's family court for the past ten years, but he had never, ever witnessed a divorce as acrimonious as *Bolger* v. *Bolger*.

Had this man and woman *ever* loved each other? he wondered as he listened to Ross Perry question a witness. It certainly seemed unlikely from the vicious, venomous charges and countercharges being exchanged today. Yet they'd been married for twelve years and had three children. They'd worked together to build a successful interior design business. All of which they were now fighting over, each and every little thing right down to ownership of the family's *TV Guide* subscription. Logan tried to picture Ned and Elaine Bolger in love with each other, sharing their hopes and plans and dreams. What had happened to that couple? What had brought them to the point where they wanted only to hurt, to destroy, each other?

Krista Conway jumped to her feet, her blue eyes flashing fire. "Your Honor, I object! Counsel is badgering the witness."

"Objection sustained," Logan said. To his surprise, the quick glance that Ross Perry gave Krista Conway was not full of emnity because she'd scored a point and he'd lost one. Rather, it was . . . admiring? And then it occurred to him. Why, these two were *enjoying* this! The acerbic volleys, the strategic moves and countermoves. Logan guessed that both Krista Conway and Ross Perry were excellent chess and tennis players, for they combined aspects of both games into their courtroom styles. With Krista Conway having the superior edge.

Logan rubbed his forehead and recalled the conversation he'd had in the courthouse earlier this morning.

"You're in for a real dogfight today," Judge Roger

Wright had warned him when the news of Judge Jack Benton's hospitalization had been announced, along with Logan's asssignment as his replacement. "The first thing on your docket is a divorce case with Conway and Perry as opposing counsel. There're always fireworks when those two sharks meet head-on."

"Fireworks?" Candace Flynn, another domestic court judge, repeated scoffingly. "You mean bloodshed, Roger. I presided over a contested divorce with Conway and Perry opposing. No wonder Jack decided he preferred ulcer surgery to appearing in court this morning."

"Do you remember who won the case?" Roger asked curiously. "Conway or Perry?"

"Oh, I remember. How could I forget *that* case? Krista Conway won it. She's a barracuda and everyone knows it, but her technique and presentation are practically flawless. She's very crafty in a straightforward, thoroughly disarming way." Candy smiled slyly. "She reminds me a lot of myself back in my bomber days."

"Candy used to be the top divorce lawyer around here before her appointment to the bench," Roger explained to Logan. "And Krista Conway picked up where she left off. Did you teach her all your old tricks, Candy?"

"That kid didn't need any help. She's a natural," Candy said admiringly. "She's incredibly thorough. And her courtroom presence borders on overwhelming!"

"She radiates charisma," Roger agreed. "That can sway you no matter how determined you are to resist."

"Krista Conway," Logan repeated. "A woman. And she's a barracuda?" He'd heard the term, of course. It referred to the high-priced, high-powered divorce lawyers who stripped their client's hapless spouse of everything. The bombers who blew away their opposition. There were no barracudas in Garrett County.

The divorce rate and the incomes there were appreciably lower than here in Montgomery County.

Candy Flynn smiled. At least Logan thought it was a smile. It was difficult to tell with the caustic Judge Flynn. "Poor Logan!" she said. "First you find a woman judge on the bench. Now you have to contend with female barracudas, too. Total culture shock, hmm?"

Roger slapped Logan heartily on the back. "Well, at least you'll have an interesting morning, Logan. Krista Conway is probably the best divorce lawyer in the area, and Ross Perry loves giving her a run for her money. You're not going to be bored."

"It's never boring to watch Krista Conway earn her two hundred fifty thousand dollars a year," Candy added. She clearly enjoyed Logan's stunned reaction to the figure.

Actually, Logan was staggered by it. Two hundred fifty thousand dollars a year? That was four times the annual amount paid him by the state of Maryland for his judicial duties. Suddenly he was very curious to see this Krista Conway, this renowned barracuda. He'd never known a woman who commanded such an incredible salary.

"I like Krista's style," Roger said. He grinned boyishly. "That sapphire-blue Bentley convertible she drives . . ." He whistled. "Now, *that's* a car!"

"She bought it because it matches the color of her eyes," Candy added with a laugh.

"I've never seen a Bentley convertible outside a showroom," Logan said slowly. Come to think of it, he'd never seen one in a showroom, either. Only in the movies. There was no Bentley dealership in all of Garrett County. There were no *Bentleys* in all of Garrett County.

"Your honor, I object," Ross Perry practically shouted, interrupting Krista Conway's interrogation of Elaine Bolger. "This line of questioning is completely irrelevant!"

Logan glanced at Elaine, who was agitatedly twisting a handkerchief as she sat in the witness stand. Krista Conway had carefully and methodically uncovered a number of glaring inconsistencies in the woman's furious accusations against her husband.

Barracuda, Logan thought. A term coined from the vicious sea creatures of the same name. Voracious. Treacherous. His gaze shifted to Krista Conway. She tilted her head slightly, and their eyes met. Her eyes, he noticed, were an extraordinary shade of blue. An alert intelligence shone in them. Logan felt as if he'd been kicked in the solar plexus.

"Objection overruled," he heard himself decree. Ross Perry frowned and Krista looked pleased.

Logan stared from one to the other. Had his ruling been correct? It was unusual—and thoroughly disconcerting—for him to second-guess himself. He was normally quite confident of his judicial decisions. Until now. Now he wasn't sure if he'd ruled in Krista Conway's favor because it was fair or because . . . when he looked at her, he felt as if his blood had caught fire.

He'd felt the same way upon seeing her for the first time in the courtroom this morning. Judges Wright and Flynn had described Krista Conway's prowess, had marveled over her salary and her English car, but had neglected to mention that she was young and beautiful with a face and a body that one might expect to see on television or in the movies, not in a court of law.

Logan had been incredulous. Krista Conway was a knockout, and he'd been unable to drag his gaze away from her. A smooth cap of raven hair framed a heart-shaped face with delicate, almost fragile features. Her cream-white coloring provided a stark contrast to the darkness of her hair. Her wide-set blue eyes, highlighted by dark, perfectly arched brows and thick, black lashes, were so vivid that the clear sapphire color was discernible even from a distance. A treacherous barracuda? Logan's senses had protested the very thought. She looked like an angel. A beautiful, sensitive angel.

His gaze had swept over her, taking in the exquisite blue silk suit that he knew cost more than any suit he'd ever owned, the immaculate white blouse and the firm thrust of her breasts beneath it. The delectable curves of her waist and hips were enhanced by the slim skirt. He even managed to note that her legs were long and well shaped, her ankles slim and delicate. She was a bit taller than average, perhaps five six, but her small-boned frame gave the illusion of petite fragility.

He'd been totally nonplussed by his reaction to her. When was the last time he had looked at a woman and felt as if he'd been poleaxed? It had certainly never been that way between him and Beverly. He and Bev had known each other all their lives. He'd loved his wife dearly, but he couldn't recall when a single look at Bev had clouded his brain. Not even Amy Sue Archer, with her blond baby-doll appeal, had triggered such a reaction in him.

Logan had continued to stare, and slowly, slowly, it dawned on him. Krista Conway held a power far more potent than her disturbing beauty. She exuded a vibrant sexuality that beckoned effortlessly. And tempted. Logan had abruptly swallowed and looked away.

Only to focus on her mouth moments later. She had a beautifully shaped mouth, enhanced by crimson lipstick. A sexy, mobile mouth that had made his pulses thunder. When her lips had parted under his gaze, he'd actually felt the effects physically. No, Krista Conway wasn't an angel. The unwelcome throbbing in his loins overturned that decision. No angel could arouse such a primitive male response. She was sexy, sultry—

"Hearsay, Your Honor. I object!" Ross Perry shouted.

Logan cleared his throat. Krista Conway looked up at him. She raised her brows and her lips twitched. "Sorry, Your Honor," she said before he had a chance to speak, sounding for all the world like a penitent schoolgirl. Except, Logan thought, that voice of hers was as sexy and sultry as the rest of her. No schoolgirl ever had a voice or a body like Krista Conway's. And no schoolgirl ever moved with her fluid grace. Her every word, her every movement was compelling. He was fascinated by her, he admitted reluctantly to himself. Watching her, listening to her was . . . exciting. And then some.

"Your Honor, may we have a five-minute recess?" Ross Perry asked. Logan wondered if Perry intuitively sensed his preoccupation with the opposing counsel, or was he simply hoping to halt Conway's momentum and bolster his agitated client? Whatever the reasons, Logan granted the delay.

Krista immediately returned to her client, while Elaine stepped down from the witness stand. Logan retired to his chambers and downed a glass of ice water. He felt out of his depth, for all his ten years' experience on the bench. This was definitely a big-city divorce trial, and the participants were a breed apart from the residents of Garrett County. Back home he'd handled all kinds of cases involving family law and had gained a reputation for innovative approaches and creative solutions. But here, now . . .

He was losing control of the case, Logan acknowledged grimly. Somehow Krista Conway had taken over, with Ross Perry figuratively snapping at her heels and the judge somewhere out in left field. He was going to end up ruling in Conway's favor and he wasn't sure how or why. What had Judge Flynn said? "She's very crafty in a straightforward, thoroughly disarming way." How true! And then Judge Wright had chimed in with, "She radiates charisma that can sway you no matter how determined you are to resist."

He was determined to resist! He'd been dazzled, Logan admitted, but not exclusively by Krista Conway. The whole scene was dazzling. The Bolgers' sophisticated city lifestyle, their income in the high six figures, complete with Porsches, valuable antiques, and annual trips to Europe, and even the hard-driving yet polished aggression of their two attorneys.

But the brief respite had allowed Logan time to put things into perspective. It was naïve to be blinded by materialism. No matter how wealthy the clients and their attorneys, *he* was the judge here, and his power was absolute. Suppose he were back in Garrett County and this divorce was being handled by local lawyers Otis Taylor and Billy Joe Lewis? As the judge, he would pay less attention to the courtroom dynamics and look carefully at the couple and their past history. He proceeded to do just that, to visualize the Bolgers as a Garrett County working-class couple. They were the parents of three young children . . . and Judge Logan Moore staunchly believed that children needed a home with two parents.

The bailiff poked his head in the door. "Your Honor, counsel are ready," he said deferentially, signaling the end of the recess.

Logan walked back into the courtroom.

Two

Five hours later, the atmosphere in the courtroom was fairly sizzling with tension. After retiring to his chambers for two hours to consider the case, Judge Logan Moore was about to rule on *Bolger* v.*Bolger*. Krista felt a familiar surge of adrenaline cause her heart to pound and her stomach to churn. She sat on the edge of her chair, alert and expectant.

"Divorce denied," Logan Moore said in a thundering voice.

For one brief moment, the courtroom was so quiet one could hear the proverbial pin drop. Krista glanced uncertainly at Ross. His expression was as dumbfounded as her own. She rose slowly to her feet. "Er, excuse me, Your Honor, but could you . . . uh, repeat that?"

"I'm refusing to grant the divorce, counselor," Logan said coolly. Krista sat back down. "And I strongly recommend that both Elaine and Ned Bolger see a marriage counselor for a period of no less than ninety days."

"*Marriage counselor?*" Both Bolgers, Krista, and Ross all chorused aloud. Their faces and their voices mirrored their total disbelief.

"This couple has had a viable marriage for twelve

years," Logan said firmly, "and there are three children to be considered, along with a family-run business." Yes, he thought, this was exactly the way he'd handled a number of divorce cases back in Garrett County. The court-ordered efforts at reconciliation had been successful, too.

"In view of everything that is at stake here," he continued, "I feel it is the court's responsibility to promote a reconciliation between Elaine and Ned Bolger." He looked sternly at the two stunned attorneys. "May I remind you both that it is first and above all the lawyer's ethical and professional duty to seek a reconciliation between the couple before beginning divorce proceedings. A duty that seems to have been neglected here."

"A reconciliation?" Ned Bolger whispered frantically to Krista. "I can't live with Elaine! She'll kill me—if I don't kill her first! Krista, do something!"

Automatically, Krista stood again. She was still reeling from the ruling. *Divorce denied.* This was the first time she'd ever heard those words in court. The Bolgers were staring at the judge as if he'd just sentenced them both to the electric chair. "Your Honor, I—I object!" Krista heard herself exclaim. "You can't do that!"

"Well, counselor, I just did it," Logan Moore replied in silken tones of disapproval. Not once during his ten years on the bench had an attorney openly challenged his ruling in court! he thought. Six-figure income and Bentley convertible aside, this *barracuda* had a helluva nerve! "I'm sorry that you don't agree with my ruling, counselor, but there is nothing you can do about it. It is interlocutory and can't be appealed."

Was he taunting her? Krista wondered, her gaze caught by the ebony fire in his eyes. In that moment they weren't lawyer and judge, but woman and man locked in a heated contest all their own.

"But it's not the way we do things here in Montgomery County," Krista hastened to explain. At once she realized she'd compounded her error. Drastically. By the expression on the judge's face, she knew he thought she was taking potshots at his own Garrett County!

"It is now, counselor." Logan's voice was heavy with sarcasm. He hadn't missed that swipe she'd taken at Garrett County. "Now, if you've finished dispensing your . . . advice to the court, perhaps you'll permit me to continue."

Humiliated and utterly impotent, Krista sank into her chair. Silence fell over the courtroom again, and she felt every eye upon her. Good Lord, what had she done?

She was appalled by her outburst. She'd never blown her cool in court—until now. The judge was absolutely right. There *was* nothing she could do about his ruling, and however much she disagreed, to challenge him so blatantly had been foolish and impulsive and . . . just plain stupid.

He'd chastised her in front of the entire court as if she were a first-year law student. And worst of all, she deserved it because she'd *acted* like a first-year law student. Out of the corner of her eye she saw Ross Perry smirking. If the judge's ruling had upset him, seeing his rival upbraided in front of the court seemed to be sufficient recompense.

Judge Moore was addressing Ned and Elaine Bolger, explaining the terms of his ruling, but Krista scarcely heard a word. She was too busy remonstrating with herself. She had always taken the utmost care not to offend the judges in family court. She had to present her cases before them, and she didn't care to go into any court fight with the judge already prejudiced against her.

And, in a strange and reluctant way, she half admired Logan Moore's courage in handing down the shockingly unexpected decree. She conceded his points—the Bolgers had once had a viable marriage, they had three children and a business between them. In a romance novel, a reconciliation would be possible, maybe even inevitable. Krista thoroughly enjoyed romance novels. After hours of listening to couples slug it out, it was refreshing and revitalizing to get lost in a world where couples loved and lived happily ever after.

But Krista never made the mistake of confusing the two worlds. And here in the real world . . . Her gaze darted from Ned to Elaine. The enmity between them was almost violently tangible. No, here in the real world, reconciliation was impossible. Judge Moore had definitely made a mistake.

It was just too bad she had told him so. She had blown it in Judge Logan Moore's courtroom. Krista was under no illusions about that! Ross Perry was well aware of it, too.

"Don't look so glum," he said cheerfully as they left the courtroom and walked into the corridor. "Moore's only substituting for Benton. It's a one-shot deal, Krista. You won't come before him again, and by the time the Bolgers refile their divorce petition, Moore will be long gone."

"No, Mr. Perry. Moore will *not* be long gone." Judge Logan Moore's deep voice sounded behind them.

Ross and Krista whirled around to find the judge standing directly in back of them. His towering height dwarfed them both. Ross's face reddened, as if he were a naughty schoolboy caught by the headmaster.

Logan continued. "I'm replacing Bill McCrory for a year on the bench here in Montgomery County," he said coolly. "He's taken a sabbatical to teach at Yale and I've been assigned to domestic court during his absence."

A year! Krista thought, stifling the urge to groan aloud. Although most of her cases were settled out of court, at least three out of ten resulted in a court fight. If she were to have the bad luck to be assigned to Logan Moore's courtroom again, she could look forward to knowing that the judge would be ninety percent against her before she even set foot in court.

"Judge Moore, I'd like to apologize," she began quickly, and made the mistake of looking up at him. She had to tilt her head because he was so tall. His ebony eyes burned into hers.

"Would you?" Logan asked. He felt his pulses quicken. She had the biggest, bluest eyes he'd ever seen.

"Yes." Krista swallowed. His rough voice indicated he didn't like her at all, and wasn't going to make it easy for her. "I was way out of line, and I really have no excuse except that you—you caught me off guard."

She wished he wouldn't keep staring at her. He towered over her, big and strong and dark, his powerful frame emphasized by the dark judicial robe. His gaze held hers for a long moment, then lingered on her mouth before dropping to her full breasts. Krista felt her nipples tingle in response, felt them tighten and thrust against the filmy material of her bra.

No, she protested to herself. She couldn't be sexually attracted to a *judge!* It was pure folly. Unprofessional and totally uncharacteristic. Exactly the way she'd been acting since she'd first laid eyes on Logan Moore this morning.

"Caught you off guard?" he repeated mockingly. "Because I didn't rule in your favor, counselor?" Logan couldn't look away from her. He was captivated by her, unwillingly so, and was furious with himself and her. Why did her eyes have to be so vividly blue, so expressively alight and alert? Why did she have to have the most kissable mouth he'd ever seen? And why did she exude a sexual radiance that was irresistibly tempting? A sharp surge of unwelcome desire surged through him.

No, he couldn't *want* her. It was absurd, impossible, and totally out of character. His tastes didn't run to rich, polished, and aggressive *feminists.* He was forty years old, a qualified and respected judge, a widower and the father of three. A man who stood for family and tradition.

He had a fiancée back in Garrett County, for Pete's sake! No, not a fiancée. Not quite. He and Amy Sue weren't officially engaged, but the subject of marriage had been tacitly implied. Hopefully by the end of this year, his children would've come to terms with him marrying again and he and Amy Sue could announce their engagement.

Yet here he stood gazing at Krista Conway like a moonstruck idiot! How she must be laughing at him. Did the lady bomber with the sapphire-blue eyes—she really drove a Bentley that same gorgeous shade?—believe she'd scored yet another kill? Did she think that the mountain-county rube would be no match for her East Coast experience and sophistication?

"I'm not bedazzled by courtroom barracudas, counselor," he said sharply. Dammit, it was true! He must take care to remember exactly what she was, despite how she looked. "I'm interested in building up rather than tearing down. And I intend to administer an antidote to the poison you inject into marriages that could be saved."

"I don't inject the poison into the marriages," Krista said, stung by his verbal blast. "It's already there, destroying the marriage long before I become involved. Sometimes *divorce* is the only antidote."

"That's exactly what I'd expect you to say, counselor. After all, you get rich on divorce, don't you?" Even as he spoke, Logan knew he was way out of line. Why was he lashing out at her this way? Ross Perry was staring at him as if he'd taken leave of his senses. Perhaps he had at that. He was ordinarily quite equanimous. Harsh confrontation simply wasn't his style.

When he looked at Krista Conway, though, something burned within him, something that grew hotter the closer he came to her. He'd never experienced such intensity, such wildness. It was alarming and . . . incredibly exciting. For the first time since Beverly's death he felt truly vital, connected to life instead of just going through the motions of living.

Krista opened her mouth to speak, then quickly closed it. She wanted to tell Judge Moore that she'd become a matrimonial lawyer because in law school she'd found the divorce laws unfair and uneven, and she wanted to equalize the disparities. Just because she possessed a definite flair for this line of work didn't mean she was antimarriage and antifamily. Far from it.

But the hard glitter in the judge's black eyes stopped her. He had already judged her. She didn't have to justify herself to Logan Moore, who'd obviously sentenced and condemned her in his mind.

"My clients come to me," she said. "I don't seek them out." She drew herself up to her full height and met his dark glare straight on. "And I'm fully aware that a lawyer is ethically obliged to suggest a reconciliation between the couple before beginning divorce proceedings. I always do. But in some cases—the Bolgers' case for one—the prospect of a reconciliation simply isn't realistic. There is too much hostility and hate between them for any love to have survived."

"Where there is hate, there is strong feeling," Ross Perry said. His smile was slightly whimsical. "And the presence of strong feelings suggests passion, however masked it might be. Perhaps the Bolgers have a chance after all."

Logan and Krista stared at each other. Ross's words—"The presence of strong feelings suggests passion"—seemed to hang in the air between them, then echo through their heads. The sights and sounds around them blurred and faded as their awareness of each other heightened and sharpened.

Krista gazed into Logan's dark, dark eyes. She

knew instinctively that he was a man used to wielding power, a man accustomed to being obeyed. He would dominate a woman, in and out of bed. Or he would certainly try to. And while she rebelled at such a notion, some primitive urge deep within her caused her to wonder what it would be like to lie pliant in his arms, to be caressed into submission by those big hands . . .

Her breath caught in her throat. She felt as if she were on the verge of losing herself in the liquid velvet lures of his ebony eyes. Why? she wondered dazedly. How?

Krista Conway was a beautiful, strong, and successful woman who could hold her own in the competitive world of men, Logan thought. She was also totally beyond the realm of his experience. He had no business being attracted to her, yet he felt himself being drawn into the compelling depths of her bright blue eyes. She looked soft and silky, and was infinitely desirable. What would it be like to have her supple body beneath him, to run his hands over her lush curves and make her cry out for a fulfillment only he could give her? To sheathe himself in her dark, moist heat? His body tightened.

Almost imperceptibly, they moved toward one another.

"If you'll excuse me, Judge Moore," Ross Perry said, "I have an appointment I'm already late for." His brisk tone abruptly snapped the sensual bond between Krista and Logan.

"Yes, of course, Mr. Perry," Logan said. A dark red stain spread from his neck to his face. Though no one could know he'd been sexually fantasizing, he was ashamed of himself nonetheless. Krista Conway made him forget all sense of time and place. That had never happened to him before, with any woman. He glared down at her and felt a sensual ache from his teeth to his heels.

"I . . . uh, have an appointment, too," Krista said quickly. She didn't, but the urge to escape from Logan Moore's engulfing black stare was overwhelming. Not that she was running away, she assured herself. But the judge did have a strangely unsettling effect on her. An effect she didn't dare examine very closely.

"Hold the elevator!" Ross called as he rushed toward the half-occupied car. Krista hurried after him. Just as she was about to step into the elevator, something—an almost tangible force—caused her to turn and look back. Logan Moore was watching her. Slowly, reluctantly, she met his eyes.

Their gazes held and locked until the elevator doors snapped shut, separating them.

"Whew! What a case!" Ross leaned back and expelled a long breath. "As if the Bolgers weren't harrowing enough, we get a judge who doesn't believe in divorce. Give me Candace Flynn in a courtroom any day. To her, divorce is a sacrament."

Krista made no reply. She was staring at the lighted numbers on the elevator's electronic panel, but she was seeing Logan's dark eyes.

"The Landau custody case is looming," Ross continued. "You don't suppose . . ." He shook his head. "Nah, it couldn't happen again. You and I as opposing counsel for two highly volatile clients and having the case reassigned to Moore? Too coincidental."

Krista forced herself to think of the Landau custody case. She was representing Marcia Landau in an effort to gain sole custody of the Landaus' five-year-old daughter, Julie. Ross Perry wanted to do the same for Gary Landau. It promised to be a bitter dispute, just as the Landau divorce three months ago had been.

"On the other hand," Ross went on, not seeming to mind Krista's lack of participation in the conversation. "There are too few family court judges, and if

Benton is out for a while and Moore is here for an entire year . . . I'd say we have a one in two or three chance of getting Moore again."

In her mind's eye, Krista saw Logan walk into the courtroom, tall and dark and impressive in his black robe. A tight knot coiled deep in her abdomen. Their eyes had met . . . he had looked at her . . . And she had felt, had wanted . . . Her cheeks flushed.

This was so unlike her. She was always self-contained, calmly in control. It was as if Logan's black-eyed gaze had penetrated the facade she presented to the world and saw the secret dreams and longings that lay deep within her.

". . . the next time you walk in Judge Logan Moore's courtroom, Krista." Ross's laughter startled her back into the present. "You fractured me when you jumped up and said, 'Your Honor, you can't do that!' " Ross laughed again. "It was all I could do to keep from laughing out loud. Watching the judge glare daggers at you restrained me. If looks could kill, you'd have bought the farm, Conway."

Ross's rather gleeful interpretation of the interaction between her and Logan Moore brought a swift and irrevocable end to Krista's daydreams about the judge. She reminded herself that his hard stares had nothing to do with secret longings and un-tapped passion, and everything to do with plain dislike and disapproval. She mustn't delude herself into thinking otherwise. Why she had done so in the first place was a disturbing mystery, for she wasn't given to weaving romantic fantasies about the men she met.

She had a quiet but pleasant social life. Her dates took her to parties and good restaurants and the theater. There was mutual respect and companion-ship, and none of the tension and effort—and passion—that characterized a so-called "meaningful relationship." It wasn't that she deliberately avoided emotional involvement; she'd simply never met the man to inspire it.

She had begun to wonder if she ever would. But today . . . today she'd met Logan Moore. Her response to him was like nothing she'd ever experienced before. And despite her best efforts to dismiss him from her mind, his burning ebony gaze continued to scorch her.

Three

Later that afternoon Krista drove her blue Bentley through the quiet, tree-lined streets of the pleasant Montgomery County suburb. Ross Perry lived three streets up from her newly purchased red-brick Colonial home. His wife was the real estate agent who'd sold her the house. It was a legal neighborhood, Calla Perry had joked. Nine attorneys and three judges lived within a fourteen-block radius. The effervescent Calla had sold houses to most of them.

Krista pulled into her driveway. She got out of the car and walked around the side of the house to survey the wildly overgrown petunia bed. She was definitely going to have to make some time to garden this weekend. She turned back to the front door just as a little girl with huge brown eyes and a thick honey-blond braid roller-skated up the sidewalk.

"Hi, Krissy!" the child called.

Krista smiled. "Hi, Lauren. How's my best friend in the neighborhood today?"

"You mean your *only* friend in the neighborhood," Lauren corrected her, grinning. It was a standing joke between them. They'd both moved into the graceful suburban neighborhood at the beginning of September, three weeks ago, Lauren just two days before

Krista. The little girl had been combing the area for potential friends, and had run across Krista searching for her wayward cat. Lauren had stopped to help, and when Ink, the big black tom, arrived home shortly afterward, Krista had invited the child inside for a snack.

Lauren had returned every day since. She seemed to possess radar attuned to the time when Krista would get home. Krista knew the child was lonely. There was a dearth of schoolchildren in this neighborhood, which consisted mainly of older couples whose children had grown and gone, and younger couples with babies and preschoolers. There were no youngsters Lauren's age, which was nine. Today.

Krista unlocked and opened the front door as Lauren slipped off her roller skates and set them neatly on the front step.

"Happy birthday, Lauren," Krista said as they entered the house. She handed the child an armful of gaily wrapped gifts that had been left on the hall table.

"Krissy!" Lauren gasped, staring at the presents in astonishment. "You remembered!"

"Do you think I could forget my only friend in the nighborhood's birthday? Go on, open them."

Lauren didn't need to be urged. She tore through the wrapping paper in a matter of seconds. "Tahitian Barbie!" she shrieked. "And Ken and Skipper. And Barbie's Pet Parrot! And—and clothes for them, too!" Clutching all the boxes, she hurled herself against Krista, who gave her a quick, laughing hug.

"Krissy, it's just what I wanted!"

"I'm glad, Lauren."

"How did you ever know?" Enraptured, Lauren dropped to the floor to examine each doll and outfit in the individual bright boxes. Tao, Krista's blue-eyed seal point Siamese cat, joined her, investigating the wrapping paper with his usual curiosity.

Krista smiled. "We lawyers are used to picking up

on verbal clues." Which hadn't been at all difficult in this case, she thought. Lauren was a chatterbox who talked freely about her life and her interests. Barbie and Ken ranked right at the top of the list.

Krista had also learned that the little girl had moved to this neighborhood with her father and teenaged brother and sister, that she'd always wanted a cat—thus her devotion to Krista's two, Ink and Tao—and that her mother had died when Lauren was five. All this had been recited matter-of-factly and in no particular order of importance.

"Guess what?" Lauren said. She had removed the small toy parrot from its box and was attempting to affix it to the perch in the bird cage that came with it. Tao pounced on the empty box.

"What?" Krista asked. She walked into the living room and removed a record from the large collection stored on the shelves beneath her stereo.

"Awful Amy Sue sent me a birthday card," Lauren said. "I ripped it up and threw it away. Look, Krissy, isn't the bird neat?"

"Neat. Why did you rip up Awful Amy Sue's card?"

Lauren frequently regaled Krista with tales of Awful Amy Sue, the apparently ghastly specter who, as the child scathingly put it, "thinks she's Daddy's girlfriend." Lauren didn't think so. From what Krista could discern, Lauren and her sister and brother were dedicated to sabotaging whatever relationship the hapless Amy Sue had with their father.

"It was the stupidest card in the world!" Lauren said scornfully. "It had a big red eight on it."

"And you're nine, of course."

Lauren nodded. "Mitch says she's a geek." Mitch was Lauren's sixteen-year-old brother. Krista had met and talked with both the sister and the brother a number of times when they'd come to fetch Lauren, though she had yet to meet the children's father.

"She probably meant well," Krista said, privately concluding that Awful Amy Sue had blown it by getting Lauren's age wrong. She set the record on the turntable and turned it on.

"We're not going to tell Daddy that she sent a dumb old card. And Denise is going to say, 'Well, you'd think Amy Sue could've at least sent Lauren a card on her birthday.' " Lauren flashed a perfectly wicked grin.

Krista knew that fourteen-year-old Denise disliked Amy Sue as intensely as Lauren and Mitch did. As a divorce lawyer, she also knew how second marriages could be disrupted by hostile stepchildren. Any possible union between these kids' father and Awful Amy Sue seemed doomed from the start.

"I like that song," Lauren said, clearly dismissing Amy Sue from her mind as she reverently removed Barbie, Ken, and Skipper from their respective boxes. "What is it?"

" 'Believe Me' by the Royal Teens. It was my brother Eric's favorite. He collected early, obscure rock and roll records and this was one of the few that I managed to save from his collection. I've been told it sells for up to ten dollars a copy—if you can even find one."

"We have lots of old records at home," Lauren said eagerly. "I like to play them."

Krista smiled rather sheepishly. "So do I." Perhaps she was a cultural deadhead, but she dearly loved those songs that brought back such fond memories of her childhood, and Eric's adolescence. They'd been close despite the seven-year age difference between them.

Lauren liked "Believe Me" so much, she wanted to play it again. And again. By the fifth time, she was singing along.

Her sister Denise called shortly afterward to remind Lauren to come home for dinner. "Krissy, will you come to my house after dinner and have some of my birthday cake?" Lauren pleaded as Krista walked her to the corner.

"If you don't think your father will mind, I'd be delighted to come, Lauren."

"Oh, Daddy won't mind. It's a very, very big cake."

Krista smiled. "Then I'll definitely be there."

"Well," Logan Moore said as he finished carving the roast chicken and passed the platter to his son, Mitch. "How did everyone's day go today?"

"Fine," chorused Mitch, Denise, and Lauren.

It was their usual response to his daily question.

"Denise, do you think you could cook something besides chicken?" Mitch asked. "This must be the third time we've had it this week." He grimaced at the platter, but still heaped his plate full. "At this rate, I'm going to sprout feathers and start to lay eggs."

"I like chicken," Denise said. "It's easy to make."

"I like chicken, too," Lauren put in loyally, although she wasn't paying any attention to dinner. She was too busy lining up three bathing-suit-clad dolls and a toy bird cage with a parrot in it.

"Er, what do you have there, Lauren?" Logan asked.

"My new dolls. My friend Krissy gave them to me for my birthday. And clothes for them too, Daddy," she added proudly.

"She gave you all that?" Logan had heard Lauren speak of Krissy, her new little friend in the neighborhood. He didn't know the child's last name, he realized. Nor had he called on her parents, which was severely remiss of him, particularly in light of their very generous birthday gifts to Lauren.

He felt acutely ashamed of himself. His child had been spending time with this little girl and he hadn't even bothered to make the family's acquaintance. Between familiarizing himself with his duties at the courthouse and settling into Bill McCrory's home— he'd been invited to use the house during his stay in Montgomery County—there simply weren't enough hours in the day. It was a lame excuse, he knew. He would call on Krissy's mother tomorrow, as soon as he arrived home.

"All the kids in my class liked the cupcakes Denise baked for my birthday, Daddy," Lauren said.

"I'm glad, Lauren. Thanks again, Denise." Logan smiled at both his daughters and felt his heart turn in his chest. He remembered the fuss Beverly had made over the children's birthdays—a party at school, another elaborate party at the house with games and favors and lots of presents, and a big beautiful cake she'd decorated herself.

Poor little Lauren had never really known any of that, though, for Bev's illness had struck when their youngest child was barely four. Ever since Lauren had begun elementary school, Denise had faithfully baked the cupcakes for her little sister's classrooom treat.

"I like my presents from Grandma and Aunt Donna and Aunt Tammy, too," Lauren said happily. "This is the best birthday I've ever had, Daddy."

Logan felt his throat tighten as he gazed at his small daughter. She looked so like her mother, with the same petite bone structure, the same wide brown eyes and thick honey-blond hair. Lauren was a survivor; she'd had to be. And she seemed a happy enough child, but he still felt she'd been short-changed.

He wanted a traditional home life for his children, the kind he'd had when he was growing up. He wanted a full-time wife and mother in his home, someone who was waiting with freshly baked cookies and milk when the children came home from school, someone who served nourishing meals. Chicken three nights a week and take-out pizza the other four weren't his idea of wholesome family dining.

He not only wanted a mother for his children, he wanted a wife, Logan thought. A sweet old-fashioned girl whose joy in life was taking care of her family. A woman like his beloved Beverly. Eight months ago, he'd found what he was looking for . . .

"Did you get anything from Amy Sue Archer, Lauren?" Mitch asked. The sound of the name of the very person he'd been thinking of jolted Logan from his reverie.

"Nope." Lauren shook her head.

"Well, you'd think Amy Sue could've at least sent Lauren a card on her birthday," Denise said with a sniff.

"Why? She hates me," Lauren said, purposefully stabbing her peas with her fork. "She hates all of us but Daddy."

"Sweetheart, that just isn't so," Logan said. "Amy Sue has told me many times how very much she cares for all three of you."

"She tells you what you want to hear, Dad," Mitch said.

Logan tensed. "Mitchell, that isn't true." Logan had thought he'd found the ideal woman to bring into his home as wife and mother, only to have his children develop an unaccountable loathing for the lovely court stenographer Amy Sue Archer.

"Let's not talk about Aw—Amy Sue," Denise said. "Just the sound of her name gives me indigestion. We're here, she's in Garrett County. Thank heavens she's permanently out of our lives."

"Denise," Logan said, "I agreed to take this one-year position as visiting judge to give Amy Sue and me time apart to think about our future. I never said that she is permanently out of our lives."

"She will be," Mitch muttered into his glass of milk. Logan pointedly ignored the comment.

Dinner continued in silence for a few minutes, then Lauren began to sing.

"Oh, no!" Denise said. "Lauren, do you always have to sing those corny moldy oldies from Daddy's collection?"

Undaunted, Lauren continued to sing. "The kid

has no taste in music," Mitch teased. "She'll probably start singing show tunes next."

"That's 'Believe Me' by the Royal Teens," Logan said. "One of the few old classic rock and roll records I don't have. Linda Payne took my copy after we broke up and swore it was hers," he added with a reminiscent grin. "It was one of my favorite records and I was never able to find another copy. Where did you hear it, Lauren? On the radio?"

"I heard it at Krissy's house today. She says it costs up to ten dollars if you can ever find a copy," Lauren said knowledgeably. She started to sing the chorus again, and Logan chimed in. Mitch and Denise groaned.

They were interrupted by the sound of the doorbell. "That's Krissy!" Lauren jumped from her chair. "I asked her to come up after dinner and have some of my birthday cake. It's okay, isn't it, Daddy?"

"Of course, sweetheart. I'm glad you thought to invite her. Now I'll have a chance to meet her and her mother." Logan followed his younger daughter to the door.

"Her mother?" Denise repeated, turning to her brother. "Krista doesn't live with her mother."

"She lives with the most gorgeous car in all of Maryland," Mitch said dreamily. "Maybe she drove it here." He leaped from his chair.

"She'd hardly drive less than two blocks," Denise said scoffingly, but she rose too and trailed into the hall after the rest of her family.

"Krissy, hi!" Lauren said joyfully.

"Did you drive, Krista?" Mitch asked hopefully.

"Those are cool shoes, Krista," Denise said.

"Happy birthday, Lauren. No, I walked, Mitch. Thank you, Denise," Krista said, in order. Then she looked up. Standing behind the children was . . . Judge Logan Moore?

Her eyes locked with his, and she felt the same peculiar surge of electricity between them that she'd experienced at the courthouse. She wasn't hallucinating. The tall, dark man standing in the hall really was Logan Moore. He was wearing a well-worn pair of jeans and a dark blue cotton shirt, the sleeves rolled up to expose the formidable muscles of his forearms. He looked as powerful and commanding as he had in his black judge's robes. And he looked incredibly, excitingly virile.

An odd tingling vibrated through her every nerve ending, and her pulses accelerated just as they had this morning when her eyes had met his. Lauren's last name was—Moore! But who would've ever made the connection? Krista ran her fingers through her hair, tousling it in her agitation. Good Lord, the judge was Lauren's father!

He looked as stunned as she felt, and she recovered first. "Hello, Judge Moore," she said politely, swiftly averting her gaze.

Logan was thunderstruck. Krista Conway! Here in his home? And she appeared to know all three of his children, and they knew her. "Are you little Krissy's mother?" he managed to ask. He'd found her stunningly attractive this morning in her expensive heather-blue suit. Now, dressed in slim cream-colored slacks, a loose-fitting dusty rose cotton sweater, and a pair of strappy, obviously expensive leather sandals, she was just as striking, just as sexy.

And she was a mother? And married? Logan frowned.

"Little Krissy?" Krista repeated, confused.

"That's you," Denise said, amusement gleaming in her dark eyes. They were just like her father's, Krista realized. "Daddy thought you were Lauren's age."

"Not hardly, Dad," Mitch drawled.

Logan cleared his throat. "I assumed Lauren's friend Krissy was a child," he said stiffly. *Krista*

Conway had befriended Lauren? What did a glamorous barracuda lawyer want with a nine-year-old? Unless . . . she knew that the child's father was a judge and hoped to curry favor with him?

Krista watched expressions ranging from astonishment to suspicion cross Logan's face. "You can forget what you're thinking, Judge Moore," she said coolly. "I had no idea Lauren's father was the visiting judge. Or a judge at all."

The only thing she'd known about Lauren's father was that he dated an apparently dreadful creature his children had dubbed Awful Amy Sue. The knowledge was strangely unsettling.

"C'mon, let's have my cake," Lauren said, taking Krista by the hand and dragging her into the dining room.

The bakery cake was decorated with pink and yellow roses. They all sang "Happy Birthday" to Lauren and applauded when she blew out the nine candles with one vigorous breath. Krista was aware of the judge's gaze on her the whole time.

He was studying her with the same concentration a bacteriologist might apply to a new virus that had turned up under his microscope. He didn't want her here in his home; he'd made his dislike of her amply evident today in the courthouse. He even had the nerve to think that she'd cozied up to little Lauren to put in a fix with him! The notion inflamed her. As far as she was concerned, Awful Amy Sue was welcome to him. And he deserved her, whatever she might be!

Determined to ignore him, she turned her full attention to Logan's children. Mitch, at six feet one, was thin, almost gangling. He had not yet gained the weight to correspond to his height. He had his father's dark hair and eyes, and his face was boyishly appealing with the promise of compelling masculinity. Had Logan looked like his son at the age of sixteen? she wondered. It was hard to picture the stern judge so youthfully vulnerable.

Denise was small and slender with shoulder-length dark hair and an ingenue appeal that was certain to bloom into real beauty. Then there was cute little Lauren, so open and friendly. Krista liked all three young Moores. It was difficult to believe they'd been spawned by the sober and severe Logan.

"Daddy, Krista is a lawyer," Denise informed her father as he silently consumed his cake.

"I know." He looked up and pinned Krista with a hard stare. "We met in court this morning."

"Hey, no kidding?" Mitch helped himself to another generous slice of the cake. "What happened?"

"That's a very good question, Mitch," Krista said. She turned to Logan. He was so disapproving, so deadpan, she couldn't resist needling him. "What *did* happen in court this morning, Your Honor? I haven't quite figured it out myself."

Logan met Krista's sparkling sapphire gaze. "Two bombers were defused. And hopefully, a marriage was saved."

"Not the Bolgers' marriage," she said. "It was over long before either Ross Perry or I came on the scene."

Clearly bored with the adult conversation, Lauren began to sing again.

"Oh, no," Mitch said with a mock groan. "There goes Lauren with another blast from the past."

"That's one of the little-known greats, 'It's Only the Beginning,' " Logan said to his son. "The Kalin Twins recorded it on the Decca label."

Krista glanced at Logan in amazement. "You sound like an avid fan of early rock and roll." Like her brother Eric had been.

"I am. My collection dates from the doo-wop era of the 1950s to the mid-sixties, when the unfortunate brainwashing of the public began with that imported English garbage."

"My brother shared your sentiments exactly," Krista said. She'd often heard Eric utter the same lament.

"Obviously a man of discerning musical taste," Logan said, nodding.

Krista thought of Eric and smiled softly. "Yes."

Logan turned his attention back to the children. "I learned how to dance the cha-cha to 'It's Only the Beginning.' "

Denise moaned. "Daddy, really! The cha-cha? How embarrassing!"

"It appears I've committed a social blunder," Logan said mildly.

"Quite a gaffe, it seems," Krista said, liking the way he didn't let his teenage daughter's criticism bother him in the least.

"Hey, Denise," Mitch said. "Remember the time Dad tried to teach us that line dance?" He snickered. "What was the name of it?"

"I don't know. It was as lame as the cha-cha," Denise said.

"The stroll." Logan's lips twitched. "It was the stroll, kids."

"I know the stroll," Krista said. "My brother nearly wore out his copy of Fabian's 'Turn Me Loose' teaching it to me."

"Who?" shrieked Denise. "What group is that?"

Krista caught Logan's eye. "This younger generation has no grasp of music history," she said mournfully, and grinned.

Her smile went to Logan's head like a straight shot of hundred-proof bourbon. On an empty stomach. "You're too young yourself to know much about Fabian and the stroll," he said dampeningly. The more irresistible he found her, the more determined he was to resist the pull of her charm. She was not his type. Not his type at all.

"I was my older brother's loyal minion," she said, "and learned all the old songs and dances from him when I was in grade school." She flashed another smile. For just a moment, she'd felt Logan Moore begin to thaw, and she wanted to continue the defrosting.

"Can you really do the . . . uh, stroll?" Mitch asked incredulously.

"Of course," said Krista. "Do you want me to teach it to you sometime?" She sent Logan an impudent, teasing glance. "Maybe your dad doesn't remember the dance well enough to teach it."

"Doesn't remember it?" he repeated. He couldn't let that one pass. "Linda Payne and I used to lead the stroll every Saturday at the local VFW teen dances."

"Show us how to do it," Denise said suddenly. "You and Krista, Daddy."

"I thought you said it was as lame as the cha-cha," Logan reminded her.

"It is. But I still want to see you do it. I'm in the mood for a good laugh," she added cheekily.

"A good laugh?" Logan stood up. "My dear child, you're going to be so awestruck by the intricacies of strolling that you'll be begging to learn it yourself." He glanced over at Krista and suddenly, inexplicably, felt lighthearted. He forgot to remind himself that Krista was not his type. "Shall we show them what they've missed by being 'Born Too Late'?"

"Definitely." She smiled at him, and that smile sent him higher.

Logan motioned the others to follow him to the family room. "We'll have to go into the archives to find the proper music," he said, and removed a number of rather dusty circular record cases from the shelves in the closet.

Krista helped him sort through the records. "You have the most extensive collection I've ever seen," she exclaimed, her eyes alight with enthusiasm. "Ones I've never heard of. And all my brother's old favorites."

"Daddy doesn't have 'Believe Me,'" Lauren piped up.

"I've been collecting for years," Logan said, "but that's one record that's eluded me." He smiled, and Krista felt a warm melting sensation in her abdomen. It was the first time he'd smiled at her, and it left her curiously breathless. He selected several records and reached for her hand. "Let's see if you're as nimble on your feet as you are with your tongue, counselor."

Which was how Logan and Krista came to spend the next hour doing the stroll to several old songs recorded exclusively for that dance back in its brief heyday. Mitch, Denise, and Lauren watched and hooted and teased as the two adults went through all the steps. They were both a bit rusty, but after a few run-throughs their timing was perfect, their movements precisely matched.

Denise and Mitch joined them, and Lauren went solo down the line. All three young Moores were quick to pick up the steps. Then Krista searched through Logan's collection of old 45's, found three venerable classics, and challenged the children to learn the cha-cha.

She and Logan showed them how. Logan kept adding additional twists and turns that totally tripped up Denise. "It's a good thing I wasn't around in your era!" she said as she collapsed on the sofa, laughing. "I'd've been a total social clod because I couldn't cha-cha. I think I'd have better luck learning the turkey trot."

"Before our time," Logan said. "Come here, counselor. Let's give them another demonstration." He caught Krista around the waist and hauled her into the middle of their impromptu dance floor. During the past hour he'd somehow forgotten that he was a conservative judge who thoroughly disapproved of her. He'd even forgotten she was not his type of woman, a high-powered divorce lawyer whose income quadrupled his. He had simply enjoyed being with her very much.

Mitch chose that moment to play one of the truly golden greats, "In the Still of the Night." It was a slow song, a dreamy anthem of old high school dances. Logan and Krista faced each other, suddenly awkward.

"Don't you old guys know how to slow dance?" Mitch asked, taunting.

"They didn't slow dance back in the olden days," Denise said. "Play another cha-cha-*cha!*"

Thanks to the children's presence, the moment of tension was slowly diffused. "We old guys *invented* the slow dance back in the golden days," Logan said. He took Krista's hand in his and placed his other hand on her waist. "Let's show 'em how it's done."

Krista laid her hand on his shoulder and looked up at him. She'd been having such a good time, listening to the old songs, dancing the old dances, and laughing with the childen, that she'd forgotten to be tense with Logan. She'd forgotten he was a judge who thoroughly disapproved of her. She'd even managed to forget that his black-eyed gaze wreaked havoc with her equilibrium.

His fingers tightened on her waist and she stumbled slightly, one of her few missteps of the evening. Logan looked down into her sapphire eyes, and a sharp pang of awareness rippled through him. She was so bright and lively. He and the children had laughed more together tonight than they had in a long time, and he knew it was Krista's vibrant charm that had made it all happen.

They'd danced together, and joked and played together, and now, touching her, holding her—even at this most discreet distance—he could feel his body hardening with desire. The subtle scent of her perfume wafted into his nostrils, her hand felt small and dainty in his. His arms tensed with the urge to pull her closer.

The sharp sexual tension between them hadn't been diffused at all. It had merely gone underground to surface at triple its former intensity.

"That's not how they dance on *American Bandstand*," Lauren called from her seat on the sidelines.

"I'll say not," Mitch agreed. "You two look like you're doing the waltz or something. Move closer. Krista should have her arms around Dad's neck, and Dad should have both arms around Krista's waist. That's how *our* generation slow dances."

She wanted to be in Logan's arms, Krista realized with a jolt. She wanted to wind her arms around his neck and run her fingers through the springy thickness of his hair, to press herself against his big, hard frame and sway to the romantic old ballad.

Logan, however, didn't dare draw Krista closer. He was already becoming aroused. If he were to hold her tight against him, he wouldn't be able to stop himself from burying his lips in the hollow of her neck and tasting the sweetness of her skin. He wouldn't be able to keep from running his hands over her body. He would *have* to feel the gentle flare of her hips, the rounded firmness of her bottom, the soft curve of her breasts. . . .

If he'd wanted her when he'd first laid eyes on her this morning, the time spent in her company tonight had intensified that desire tenfold, until it toppled perilously close to "need." With a stifled groan, Logan deliberately widened the distance between them. His three children were present, for heaven's sake! And they were all eyes and ears!

"The phone's ringing," Lauren sang out at that moment, and scrambled to the kitchen to answer it.

"I'll get it, Lauren!" Denise was hot on her trail.

"It could be for me, you know." Mitch followed them out of the room.

"That's the difference between our age and theirs,"

Krista said, smiling unsteadily. "When my phone rings at home, I groan at the intrusion. They beat a path to answer it."

Lauren marched back into the room just then with the air of one determined to complete an important assignment. She switched off the lights and ran away giggling.

The record continued to play as Krista and Logan stood in the darkened room, the light from the hall casting dim shadows on the wall. They were alone, holding each other. The slow music, the darkness, the children's collective departure . . . They were alone, in the still of the night.

Four

It was all so contrived, such an obvious setup, Krista began to laugh. "Kids are *so* subtle," she said.

Logan immediately dropped her hand and moved away. "I'm sorry. This is . . . very embarrassing. I assure you this is the first time the kids have ever"—he swallowed—"done anything like this."

He walked briskly to the light switch and seconds later the room was flooded with light. "I don't know what prompted them to do it," he muttered. He was mortified. Had the children somehow divined what he was feeling as he held Krista in his arms? No, that was impossible. He had been completely circumspect. "I'm terribly sorry," he said again.

"Don't apologize." Krista grinned. Somehow his extreme discomfort eliminated any traces of her own. She felt totally in command of the situation, and was suddenly possessed by an impish determination to lord it over him. "This comes as quite a surprise after their determined opposition to Amy Sue."

His jaw dropped. "Y-You know about Amy Sue?" he managed to say in a choked voice.

"The kids have . . . um, mentioned her to me." Krista couldn't help but smile. He looked horrified, like a teenage boy whose mother had just found his secret cache of girlie magazines.

"What have they told you about her?" he asked tightly.

"Probably just what they've told you."

"Amy Sue Archer is a perfectly proper, sweet, and well-brought-up young lady."

"They forgot to tell me that."

Her teasing grin inflamed him. "She's a lovely girl."

Krista remembered Denise's description of Awful Amy Sue. "She looks about as real as one of Lauren's Barbie dolls. Big bazooms and teensy little waist. Long white-blond hair that she's always throwing around. And the fakest, phoniest smile you've ever seen." Krista raised her brows. "I did hear she was rather attractive." If you liked Barbie-doll looks and fake, phony smiles.

"I simply can't understand why the children have taken such an intense dislike to Amy Sue." Logan strode to the window and peered outside, jamming his hands into the pockets of his jeans. "She's an old-fashioned, family-centered girl with no aspirations for a career. She wants to quit her job as a court stenographer as soon as she marries, and devote herself to her husband and family. She never wants to work again."

"You don't suppose she's simply looking for a meal ticket?"

"Meal ticket?" Logan whirled around to face her, his expression revealing his outrage. "Are you implying that she views *me* as a—a *meal ticket*?"

"I didn't mean it personally," Krista said hastily. "I was just playing devil's advocate. It's a natural role in my profession. I've handled quite a few divorces where the couples are splitting because the wife had no interests of her own, no life of her own, once the wedding ring was on her finger, and the husband felt suffocated or bored with her. It's as if after saying 'I do,' she decides to do nothing. And in virtually every case like this, the man is highly intelligent and successful in his profession—a man like you."

"You have no idea what kind of a man I am! Or what I want from a woman."

She regarded him thoughtfully. "I would wager a guess that what you think you want from a woman isn't necessarily what you need."

"I know a success-oriented woman like yourself can't fathom any woman wanting to spend her life caring for a family," he said, glowering at her.

"Can't a woman be success-oriented and caring at the same time?"

He didn't answer her question. He knew what the correct response would have to be and he didn't want her to score another point off him. So he chose the time-honored counterattack as his reply. "You're ambitious. You're aggressive and highly driven. You make the kind of money that most *men* will never earn."

"You make it sound like a crime," she said dryly.

"Your career will always come first with you. Isn't that why you're not married?"

"But of course. A man-eating barracuda like me scares the fish . . . uh, I mean, men away." Her sapphire-blue eyes sparkled with amusement and her smile taunted him. "Why, I eat inexperienced guys like you for breakfast!"

"In-inexperienced!" he spluttered. "I was married at twenty-one! I've fathered three children! I'm hardly inex-ex-perienced!" His tongue tripped over the word, he was so incensed.

"You're inexperienced if you blindly pigeonhole women into one-dimensional categories. You're inexperienced if you see everything in terms of black and white with no areas of gray."

"You're quite facile with words, counselor."

"Mmm-hmm. I love to argue." There was a wicked glint in her eyes. "And naturally, I love to win the argument."

Logan knew she was laughing at herself, and was cheerfully inviting him to laugh along with her. He remembered the way she'd smiled in court, so polite and proper, while her blue eyes danced with pure deviltry. There was humor underlying whatever aggressive tactics she might employ. She was likable, no matter what she said or how far she pushed. Whereas others might provoke anger, she was unbelievably effective in making her point because she never came across as meanspirited or hostile.

Was the warmth she projected real? he wondered. Whether it was or not, it was extremely effective. And dangerous. How did a judge rule against her? How did a man resist her?

Logan's mouth tightened into a thin straight line. He *had* to resist her. He rallied his defenses to do so. "A woman like you could never be expected to understand the appeal a sweet, old-fashioned girl like Amy Sue holds for a man."

Even as he spoke of Amy Sue's appeal, he realized he had never looked at the pretty blond stenographer and felt his body go up in flames and burn the way he was burning now. The way he burned every time he looked at Krista Conway. The unwelcome knowledge infuriated him. "She's refreshingly traditional," he went on. "She's a twenty-two-year-old virgin who—"

"A twenty-two-year-old-virgin?" Krista repeated, her eyes widening. She quickly turned away.

Logan's dark brows pulled together into a V above his eyes. Three giant strides took him across the room to her side. His hand closed over her shoulder, and he spun her around to face him. "You're laughing!" he accused her.

"I . . . um, was just thinking of a joke Ross Perry told me the other day," she said quickly, but despite her best intentions, she chuckled again.

"You're laughing at *me*!"

"No, no."

"You are!" He was sure of it. Her sapphire eyes were bright with amusement. Her smiles had a devastating impact on him, but when she laughed she was postively breathtaking. Logan felt the air whoosh out of his lungs in one gasp. "Dammit, you *are* laughing at me!"

"Do you think I'm crazy? Would I laugh at a judge? One who holds the absolute power of decision over my cases?"

"You're not laughing at *Judge* Moore, the domestic court justice, you're laughing at *Logan* Moore, the man." His voice was suddenly husky. Of their own volition, his hands curved around her upper arms. He held her firmly in front of him, his black eyes blazing.

"I guess I am." Krista moistened her lips with her tongue, the small action unconsciously provocative. "Sorry."

The sight of her small pink tongue flicking over her lips had had an effect deep in Logan's loins. His fingers tightened on her arms. She was so close, and felt so small and soft beneath his hands.

She grinned up at him. "I was just trying to imagine how a man of your age—and experience—could possibly relate to a twenty-two-year-old virgin. She's a generation removed from you, a contemporary of Mitch and Denise, actually. What on earth would you have to talk about?"

Logan grimaced. He was sensitive about the age difference between him and Amy Sue. And their lack of a common ground or interests had been a sore point with him before he'd convinced himself that her traditional values and eagerness to stay at home with a family were enough for him.

"What she considers history," Krista said, "you lived as current events. When your son was born, she was in the first grade."

She'd hit a nerve, the wretched little barracuda, he thought, glaring down at her. But then, she'd been trained to go for the jugular. She got paid—handsomely—for it. "It's none of your business, counselor," he growled.

"But marriage is my business, in a reverse sort of way. What draws people together, what holds them together, and what ultimately breaks them up have always been a source of fascination for me." She looked speculatively at him. "I think I've figured out what brought you and Amy Sue together. You want a wife at home, and she wants to get married and quit work."

He muttered a curse and gave her a small shake. "If you use the word 'meal ticket' one more time, I'll—"

"I didn't say it this time."

"You implied it, Bomber Lady."

"Objection, Your Honor. That's conjecture on your part."

He almost smiled. She was laughing at him again, the blue-eyed witch. If he'd been in court, he probably would've ruled the way she wanted on the objection. Oh, she was dangerously effective, all right.

"And now," she said, "we come to what'll hold you and Awf—uh, Amy Sue together."

Why was she doing this? a sane little voice in her head asked. She was flirting with a judge, challenging him . . . on a sexual level. This was totally out of character for her. She preferred dealing on a forthright, person-to-person basis, with no allusions, veiled or otherwise, to sex. But with Logan Moore . . .

Krista felt herself getting lost again in the dark depths of his eyes. Somehow that little shake he'd given her had brought her closer to his powerful body. She inhaled his clean, masculine scent. She was achingly aware of every breath he took because her own breathing had become labored and shaky. She felt small and soft and vulnerable. Perhaps that was why she was playing the role of flirtatious female. He made her feel so aware of her sex, and the differences between them.

She drew in a jagged breath. She'd never felt sexier or more feminine in her entire life.

"Well?" he asked. His head had lowered slightly, bringing his mouth nearer to hers. "Aren't you going to tell me what will hold Amy Sue and me together?"

His voice was mocking her, she thought. Did he know what she was feeling? Did it amuse him to watch her melting for him while he blithely spoke of another woman? Krista's eyes darkened to a stormy blue.

"Damned if I know what will hold you and a twenty-two-year-old virgin together," she said with a nonchalance totally at variance with the way she was feeling. "We've already ascertained that you have nothing to say to each other. Sexual passion, perhaps? No, that couldn't be it. If there were any passion in your relationship, sweet Amy Sue wouldn't still be a virgin and you wouldn't be hundreds of miles away from her."

Logan tensed. Once again Krista had hit on a profoundly jarring truth. He'd kissed Amy Sue, but hadn't felt any real desire to advance the relationship physically. Nor had he received anything but a perfunctory response from her. But to listen to Krista Conway blatantly announce it as a bald fact ignited his temper, which had been smoldering in the embers of his control.

"What could a sharp-tongued lady barracuda possibly know about sexual passion?" he asked, glowering down at her. Suddenly they were standing so close that a sheet of paper couldn't have been slipped between them. His mouth was hovering inches above hers. "My guess is, not a damn thing!"

"Don't I?" Her voice was thick and husky, and the sound of it made him throb. Their thighs brushed.

"What *do* you know?" he asked. His lips moved closer with each softly spoken word. "Show me."

Krista inhaled shakily. "Logan," she said in a voice she hardly recognized as her own. It was full of want and need, yet soft with surrender. Her heart was hammering wildly against her ribs, and she fought to keep her eyelids from drifting shut. She wasn't prepared for the urgency that spun through her, for the wave of desire that sent her reeling. He was going to kiss her, and she wanted him to, far too much.

His big hand curved around the nape of her neck while the other rested lightly on her hip. Slowly, tentatively, he touched his mouth to hers. "Krista," he murmured as he tasted her lips. It was the first time he'd actually called her by her name, and a foolish thrill rippled through her.

He nibbled on her lower lip, then the upper one. Krista trembled, and a tiny moan escaped from deep in her throat. She closed her eyes and slid her arms around his neck, bringing her body more fully against his.

Logan's arms circled her then, pulling her into the hard planes of his body, fitting her soft curves to him as his mouth closed fiercely over hers. She parted her lips for him, and when his tongue surged inside, she made a small, soft sound and clung to him. She felt his tongue probe the inner softness of her cheeks and glide over her teeth, then rub sensuously against her own tongue, probing, tasting, enticing and exciting her.

Desire flooded her. Her bones seemed to melt. Her tongue slid into his mouth to engage in an erotic little duel with his. Her analytic lawyer's mind, which had always enabled her to remove herself from a situation while she sized it up, spun into incoherence as she plunged into a whirlpool of sensations. The erotic warmth of his caressing hands over her back. The thrust of his tongue into her mouth. The tingling of her breasts pressed against the solid wall of his chest.

His hands moved lower and his fingers clenched the rounded firmness of her buttocks, kneading and squeezing, then finally arching her into the hard cradle of his thighs. She pressed against his burgeoning heat, empty, aching, craving to be filled.

The urge to touch him was irresistible. Her hands found their way under his shirt, and she felt the hard muscles of his back beneath her fingers. His skin was warm and slightly damp, and she lightly scored it with her nails. Logan drew a sharp, rasping breath. He was so big, so strong, that she felt overpowered by his masculinity, yet infinitely drawn to him by a primal need she had never before experienced. She felt she could lose herself in him, drown in the scent and the taste and the feel of him.

His mouth left hers to move voraciously along the curve of her neck. The sharp nip of his teeth and the rough velvety texture of his tongue on her sensitive skin sent her soaring higher.

I want him. Her whole body vibrated with the urgency of that realization. She knew she had never wanted a man the way she wanted Logan. Her silent admission was enough to shock her back to sanity. Desperately, with unexpected force, she wrenched herself out of his arms.

For what seemed to be forever, they stood looking at each other, their breathing ragged, both pairs of eyes glazed and clouded with arousal. Krista was trembling with reaction, shaken by the force of her unslaked passion. She wanted him—and it was a totally impossible situation. He was a judge and she was an attorney in the same court, and a sexual relationship between them would positively scream conflict of interest. Of course, a change of venue would alleviate that, but the conflict between them ran deeper than the legal and ethical ones.

Logan Moore heartily disapproved of her, as a lawyer and as a woman. He thought she was a money-hungry, hardened automaton who was incapable of caring about anything other than her high-income-producing caseload. He might want her—his impassioned response to her tonight proved that—but he didn't *want* to want her. He didn't even want to like her!

Logan stared down at Krista, his body hard and tight, his blood pounding in his head. Never had he been so stirred by a kiss. He wanted her, wanted her with a ferocious urgency that rocked him. She'd been so passionate and pliant in his arms, he'd lost his head. He'd swiftly reached the point where kissing wasn't enough. He'd wanted to feel her bare skin under his hands, wanted to delve beneath the barrier of her clothing and touch her intimately . . .

He dragged his gaze away from her. She was wrong, all wrong for him. Apart from the ethical conflict of interest between judge and practicing attorney, they were polar opposites in everything from backgrounds to lifestyles. She was the quintessential urbanite, he was a country judge. She earned her living on the other side of the bench from him, tearing apart what he dedicated his career to preserving.

Say something! Krista told herself. She frantically cast around in her mind for some appropriately light and witty comment to break the sexual tension that ensnared them. She could think of nothing. The passion that had burned between them wasn't funny or trivial, to be dismissed with a little sophisticated repartee. It was elemental and . . . wondrous. Her cheeks flamed. Was she reacting like a schoolgirl? For the first time in her life, she was truly speechless.

Finally she swallowed and managed to speak. "I—I think I'd better leave," she murmured in a husky voice that sent another fierce jolt of desire rippling through Logan.

"And I'd better take a cold shower."

His suggestive remark drew her gaze to the evidence of his arousal, which his well-worn jeans served to accentuate. His gaze followed hers. "Yes, counselor, Exhibit A. Proof of the effect you have on me."

A surge of heat suffused her body. She knew he resented his attraction to her, as well as the passion that had flared so spontaneously and inexplicably between them. "And you don't like it," she said. It was absurd to feel hurt by his attitude toward her, but she did.

He sat down, and his lips twisted into a grim smile. "It's certainly inopportune, with three kids just a room away."

His implication—that if the children weren't present, they would've proceeded inevitably to bed—disturbed her. There had been no whispered words of endearment, no pretense of caring, of respect, or even liking! His implication was an insult, and infuriated her.

"It wouldn't matter if the children were a thousand miles away," she said hotly. "This interlude—this mistake!—wouldn't have gone any further than it did."

"Counsel is perjuring herself. Luckily, you aren't under oath."

"I don't want you!" She flung the statement at him, knowing it was a lie but determined to make it the truth. "What would I want with a man who fancies bubble-headed young virgins?"

He laughed harshly. "An impressive exit line, counselor." She'd better take the hint and leave, he thought, or she was going to find herself yanked down onto his lap, despite the kids' inhibiting presence. Arguing with her was as stimulating as kissing her.

Krista took the hint. Lifting her chin, she swept from the room, making an exit impressive enough to match the line. Halfway down the hall, she collided with Mitch, Denise, and Lauren.

"You aren't leaving, are you, Krista?" Denise asked in dismay.

"Yes, honey. It's getting late and we've all got to get up early tomorrow." Krista softened her brisk tone with a smile.

"Early to bed and early to rise," Logan said, and she started at the sound of his voice. He had joined them in the hall and moved to stand directly behind her. "Very commendable, Miss Conway."

He was too close, Krista thought. If she were to step back just an inch or two, her body would be touching his. Slowly, deliberately, she edged away from him.

"Who was on the phone?" Logan asked his children, moving toward Krista just as slowly and deliberately as she was inching away from him.

The three young Moores exchanged uneasy glances.

"Oh, uh, nobody," Denise said vaguely.

"Nobody? It was a wrong number?" Logan asked.

"Boy, was it ever!" Mitch muttered.

Krista stared from Mitch to Denise to little Lauren, who was grinning mischievously from ear to ear. Krista was especially adept at detecting the truth. She had to be because certain clients tended to embellish upon it for their own benefit, and for her to be caught without the true facts would spell doom for her case in a courtroom. At this moment she would bet her Bentley that the nobody who'd called, that wrong number, had been none other than the controversial Amy Sue Archer.

"Oh, well," Logan said, dismissing the incident.

Krista tightened her jaw. It was none of her business that Logan Moore's children and twenty-two-year-old Amy Sue were engaged in a war, and that the young Moores had clearly won this battle. *More power to them!* cheered a renegade voice within her, which she swiftly sought to suppress.

"Good night, kids," she said, and smiled, hoping she sounded sufficiently cheerful. "Thanks for the cake. And happy birthday again, Lauren."

Lauren threw her arms around Krista's waist. "Thank *you*, Krissy!"

Krista hugged her back, fully aware of Logan's ebony gaze boring through her. He probably didn't want the wicked barracuda to touch his child. He certainly wouldn't credit her with having a genuine affection for the little girl. But she did. And Lauren knew it, even if her prejudiced, chauvinistic father didn't.

"Yo, Krista," Mitch said as she stepped out onto the small front porch. "I'll walk you home."

"Thanks, Mitch, but I'll be fine on my own."

"You shouldn't be walking around alone at night," Denise said. "We don't even do that in Garrett County."

The telephone rang again, and Lauren raced to answer it. "Mitch!" she bellowed seconds later. "It's for you. Some guy named Jason."

"Probably Jason Danvers. He said he'd call me about trying out for the basketball team. Krista, wait just a few minutes and I'll be off the phone and will walk you home." He hurried off to take his call.

"It's very sweet of Mitch to offer," Krista said, "but I'll be perfectly safe walking home by myself." She started down the front walk despite protestations from Denise and Lauren.

"Wait a minute," Logan said gruffly. Krista kept on walking. "The kids are right. A woman shouldn't run around alone at night."

"Have no fears on my behalf, Your Honor," she said over her shoulder. "Surely no one would be foolhardy enough to attack a terrifying barracuda. One look from me should have even the most determined molester quaking in his shoes."

"You're the one who's foolhardy, counselor." His voice sounded in her ear just as his hand closed around her wrist. "And stubborn, too."

She tried to shake him loose. "My house is only two blocks from here and I don't want you to—"

"I'd wager a guess that what you think you want isn't necessarily what you need," he drawled in a mocking paraphrase of her own words to him. "Come on." Still holding her wrist, he hauled her along with him. "Do we make a right or left turn at the corner?"

"Neither. We keep on walking straight."

He was certainly in a hurry to get her to her door and relieve himself of his self-imposed duty, Krista thought. He walked so swiftly, his long legs taking brisk giant strides, she had to run to keep up with him. Neither spoke until Krista, breathless from the exertion, pointed out her house.

"Thank you for seeing me safely home, Judge Moore," she said with impeccable politeness as she attempted to reclaim her wrist from his manaclelike grip.

He did not release her. "You called me Logan a few minutes ago."

His tone, mocking, challenging, *seductive*, caught her completely unaware so her gaze flew to his face. He was staring down at her, watching her intently, his eyes . . . hungry. Her breath caught in her throat.

"Logan, I don't think—"

"I seem to be having the same trouble," he cut in. "Thinking, that is. You have an uncanny ability to short-circuit my common sense." His gaze lowered to his fingers, which encircled her slender wrist. "Common sense tells me to bid you good night and walk home."

"Yes, that's quite sensible," she said, and tried to pull out of his grasp. "Good night, Judge Moore."

"Ah, but the fuse has been blown on my common sense, remember?" His eyes burned into hers. "Invite me inside, Krista."

Five

Krista's heart jumped. "Not tonight, Your Honor." She wished her voice were steadier, that her pulses weren't racing.

"Why not, counselor?" Logan's big hand cupped her chin and tilted her head back, forcing her eyes to meet his.

The humor in his voice, the undisguised passion in his dark eyes, the warmth of his fingers as they stroked the curve of her neck held her in momentary thrall.

"We both know why not," she said, and pulled away from him. She took a deep breath, trying to force herself to think rationally. It wasn't easy to be logical when her every instinct urged her to go to Logan, when her senses were rioting for the pleasure she knew she would find in his arms. "Professional ethics aside, you think I'm a heartless barracuda who enjoys tearing families apart. You think I delight in making a lot of money from other people's misery."

"And you think I'm a tyrannical country bumpkin bent on imposing my hopelessly unsophisticated edicts upon your high-paying clients," Logan said.

But she had responded passionately to him, he

reminded himself. He was still slightly stunned by that fact. Krista was unlike any woman he'd ever met. She intrigued him, fascinated him. He was more than a little bit awed by her—and he'd made her want him! The realization sent a heady wave of cocky male confidence surging through him.

"No, you're wrong," she said. "I don't think you're a country bumpkin." *He* didn't refute *her* allegations, she noted. She tried to tell herself she didn't care, but she knew she was lying. For reasons that she didn't wish to analyze, Logan Moore's opinion of her mattered very much.

"The barracuda and the bumpkin," he said, and laughed slightly. "A terribly mismatched pair, I agree." *He'd made her want him.* He was half-drunk on the notion. "But you want me," he added boldly.

She was silent for a long moment, and his confidence began to falter. "You want me," he repeated. "Don't you?"

"I shouldn't," she said softly.

"But you do." He studied her carefully. He had to have her, he decided. Now. Tonight. Although he wasn't a believer in one-night stands, he needed one with Krista to exorcise her from his system. Didn't fascination, unchecked, develop into obsession?

He didn't dare develop an obsession for a woman who was not at all what he and his children needed in their lives. Taking Krista Conway to bed would satisfy his sexual curiosity, Logan assured himself. Taking her to bed would purge him of this desire, this unaccountable need for her . . .

A need which seemed to grow more intense by the minute. "I want you, Krista," he said huskily.

Krista felt weak. He said he wanted her. She caught herself staring at him and dragged her gaze away. What she had said only a few moments earlier still held. They were wrong for each other. But as he seemed likely to persist, she attempted to divert him another way. "Logan, I have to be in court tomorrow."

He looked thoughtful. "Do you always abstain from sex the night before a courtroom appearance?"

She thought he was being sarcastic, but his tone wasn't caustic. He was serious and genuinely curious, she realized, and suppressed a groan. "Naturally, Logan. Just like an athlete before a big game. We barracudas follow a similar training routine."

"I see."

"Logan . . ." Wouldn't he be surprised, she mused, if she were to tell him that her abstention from sex had nothing to do with courtroom performance and everything to do with her need for love to make the act meaningful? She hadn't been in love for a long, long time.

"Oh, what's the point?" she murmured, and sighed. He probably wouldn't believe her anyway. Logan's preconceived notion of the successful professional woman was set like cement in his mind, and it clearly included a willingness to indulge in casual sex. "Good night, Logan," she said firmly.

"I'll see you in court tomorrow, counselor."

No, it wasn't possible. "My case has been assigned to Judge Wright."

"Life is full of little surprises, isn't it, Ms. Conway? Roger Wright asked me to take his new cases tomorrow, so he could schedule an emergency dental appointment. Of course, I agreed. And imagine how surprised *I* was when I saw who was coming up before me."

"And—and knowing that you kissed me tonight and tried to hustle me into bed, anyway?" Krista was appalled. "Good Lord, what if I had gone to bed with you? How could you have sat on the bench and made an impartial ruling after—after—"

"I assure you that your skill in bed wouldn't have influenced me in the courtroom, counselor. Either way."

"You're damn right it wouldn't have! The day hasn't come when I have to sleep with a judge in order to win a case. And it never will!" She shoved her key into the lock and pushed open the door. "Good night, Judge Moore."

Logan had once read that divorces weren't won. Rather, they were lost by the side that made the most mistakes. In the case of *Marshall* v. *Marshall*, mistakes were the order of the day. James Fleener, counsel for Wilson Marshall, was practically handing victory to Krista Conway, whose thorough, flawless representation of Alice Marshall made the opposing side appear all the worse.

Krista had done her detective work well and uncovered hidden assets that had not been voluntarily disclosed. She'd called in a forensic accountant who had analyzed Wilson Marshall's business interests, and an actuary to evaluate Marshall's retirement plan. She methodically cited Alice Marshall's contribution to the twenty-eight-year marriage and gave an impassioned speech on the tragedy of displaced homemakers.

The bailiff could've settled this case, Logan thought. He watched and listened to Krista, observing her skill and expertise with purely professional admiration. Personal feelings didn't enter in it. There was only one way to rule on *Marshall* v. *Marshall*. Judge Moore awarded Alice Marshall everything her attorney had asked for her.

Denise and Lauren came to visit shortly after Krista arrived home that afternoon. She made microwave popcorn for a snack and French-braided the girls' hair while they chatted about school and television programs and records and, yes, Amy Sue Archer.

"I can't believe," Denise said, fuming, "she had

the nerve to call back last night after Mitch told her Daddy was out on a date. And Daddy answered the phone before we had a chance to get it again."

That would've been when Logan had returned after taking her home, Krista thought. "Was he . . . uh, glad to talk to her?" she couldn't resist asking, much to her self-disgust.

"I don't know," Denise said. "But there was no way we could let Daddy talk to the poisonous old witch. Lauren had to pretend she was sick."

Lauren clutched her stomach and began to roll around on the floor. "My tummy hurts! I'm going to throw up! Help!" she bellowed at the top of her lungs.

"It would be hard to carry on a romantic conversation with that racket going on," Krista said dryly.

"Yeah!" Lauren grinned, her suffering instantly ended.

"So Awful Amy Sue was foiled again." Krista frowned thoughtfully. "But what if your father really wants to marry her, kids? Do you think it's fair to sabotage his chances for happiness simply because you three don't . . . care for the woman?"

"Daddy could never be happy with Amy Sue," Denise said confidently. "If he marries her, we'll have to go live with Grandma and he would be miserable without us."

"Awful said we'd have to go," Lauren added, nodding. "She hates us as much as we hate her."

"Amy Sue told you this?" Krista was horrified. "She said you couldn't live with your father if she married him? Does your father know this?"

"Grandma told us not to tell him," Denise said. "She said to give Daddy time to come to his senses, and if he didn't realize in a while what Amy Sue is really like then she'd tell him herself. So we decided to help Daddy come to his senses a little faster, that's all."

"You like our dad, don't you, Krissy?" Lauren asked bluntly.

Krista saw the turn the conversation was about to take and quickly diverted it. "Oh, no, don't drag me into it. I'm sure your father will come to his senses on his own, without any help from me." She glanced at her watch. "Now, if you'll excuse me, I have to take a shower and wash my hair. I have a date tonight."

"A date?" Lauren echoed. She scowled and her hand went to her stomach. "I feel—"

"You feel fine." Krista laughed and impulsively hugged the child. "I've seen your act, remember?"

Denise smiled. "I think it's cool that you have a date, Krista. What's his name? Is he cute? Do you like him a lot?"

"His name is Jeremy Litman and I suppose he is cute, Denise." Krista grinned. "But I hardly know him. We met at a bar association meeting and he asked for my phone number. This is our first date. I'm expecting him to call shortly for directions to the house."

"We'll stay and answer the phone for you while you're in the shower," Denise offered sweetly.

"Would you?" Krista said just as sweetly. "I'll only be a few minutes. If he calls, come get me out of the shower." She smiled at the two girls. They smiled back.

She emerged from the shower ten minutes later and slipped on her powder-blue cotton robe. Denise and Lauren joined her in the bedroom to watch as she applied her makeup.

"I love the way you do your eyes, Krista," Denise said admiringly. "Would you do mine sometime?"

"All you need is a little eye shadow, Denise. Fourteen-year-old girls who paint themselves up with a lot of eyeliner and mascara look like junior hookers."

"You sound just like Daddy." Denise helped herself to the sea-green eye shadow. "Doesn't she, Lauren?"

Lauren nodded.

"Well, you ought to listen to your father," Krista said firmly. "He's a very wise man. Simply because a python like Amy Sue has him in her grip doesn't mean he doesn't know what's best for you kids." She glanced at her watch. "Jeremy should've called by now. You two didn't intercept his call while I was in the shower, did you?" she added teasingly.

Denise and Lauren laughed good-naturedly, not at all offended by her playful accusation. "The phone didn't ring once, Krista," Denise said. "C'mon, Lauren, we'd better get home for dinner."

"What are we having?" Lauren asked.

"Leftover chicken. I'm going to mix it with a package of Tuna Helper. You know, substitute the chicken for tuna."

"Oh, gross! I really am going to be sick!"

"Me, too. I hate to cook." Denise glanced at Krista, who was watching them with amusement. "Do you like to cook, Krista?"

"Yes, I do." She laid a hand on each girl's shoulder and walked them downstairs. "And if I weren't going out with Jeremy Litman, I'd show you something better to do with your leftover chicken."

What had happened to Jeremy? Krista wondered a few hours later. She walked to the bay window in the living room and peered out. It was nearly nine o'clock, she was starving, and Jeremy Litman still hadn't called. She frowned and sighed impatiently. She could understand if he were working late, but couldn't he at least have had the courtesy to tell her he would be delayed?

At nine-forty, she made herself a sandwich. At ten, she got ready for bed. She'd been stood up! What an inconsiderate creep Jeremy Litman was!

She watched the news on the local Metromedia station, then decided to go to bed. As she was turning down the covers, she noticed the small trimline phone on the floor—with the receiver off the hook!

She stared at it in dismay. How long had it been off the hook? Had Jeremy been trying to call her all evening, only to get a busy signal? He would have no other way to get in touch with her. Since she'd recently moved, her new address wasn't yet in the phone book, and the directory assistance operators didn't give out such information.

Tao joined her on the bed with a meow. "Did you do this?" Krista asked the Siamese crossly. She'd once seen the ever curious cat investigate the phone as it sat on the nightstand. He'd nudged the receiver off the hook and been so unnerved by the dial tone that he'd run off. "Did you knock the phone off the nightstand, Tao?" Tao meowed and began to purr.

Krista sighed. "Jeremy Litman is probably thinking *I'm* an inconsiderate creep. Shall I call him and explain what happened?"

She decided that she'd better, and then was sorry she had. Jeremy Litman subjected her to a tirade of frustrated fury, refusing to see even a bit of humor in the situation. Krista decided she'd rather not date anyone who reacted so violently to a simple mishap, and told him so. Jeremy hung up on her.

"How was your date last night, Krista?" Denise asked the next afternoon. She and Lauren had arrived shortly after Krista's return home from the office.

Krista grimaced. "Don't ask. The evening was a disaster, and we never even went out."

Lauren beamed. "Oh, too bad."

"Will you be seeing him again?" Denise asked.

Krista shook her head. "Not a chance."

Denise and Lauren exchanged pleased little smiles. Krista chewed her lower lip thoughtfully. The young Moores didn't hesitate to subvert Amy Sue's calls to their father. Was it possible . . . ?

"Krista," Denise said quickly. "Remember last night you said you could show us something better to do with leftover chicken? Well, we still have the leftover chicken. Daddy took us out for hamburgers last night instead. Would you come over and help me make dinner tonight? Please?"

Lauren caught Krista's hand in her own small one. "Oh, please, come, Krissy!"

Krista considered it, then smiled at the girls. "Oh, well, why not?"

She would show Denise how to make a chicken, rice, and vegetable casserole and then leave—long before Logan got there. The casserole was in the oven and she was ready to go home when Mitch engaged her in a discussion about college SAT's. He was planning to take them and wanted her comments on the test. Then Lauren dragged her to her room to show off all her Barbie dolls.

When Logan walked in the door Krista was still there. He stared at her. She was wearing a lavender blouse and designer blue jeans, and he thought she looked beautiful. Sexy and desirable. He remembered how her lips had felt on his. He remembered the taste and the delicious feminine scent of her. He swallowed hard.

"Krista fixed dinner for us," Denise announced. "Tell her she has to stay and eat with us, Daddy."

"I really must go," Krista said, steeling herself against the children's noisy protests.

Logan had spent entirely too much time that day thinking about Krista, and he'd vowed to put her out of his mind. He now reminded himself of that vow. "I insist that you stay and have dinner with us," he heard himself say. Where had that come from? "We won't take no for an answer."

Dinner was delightful. The casserole was delicious, the children were talkative and amusing, and Krista thoroughly enjoyed herself. So did Logan. Krista's company exhilarated him, and it was a pleasure to watch her easy interaction with his children.

At the end of the meal, Mitch stood up and said, "Denise and Lauren and I will take care of the dishes and clean up the kitchen. You two go on into the family room and play some oldies, dance, relax." He grinned at his sisters. "Enjoy yourselves."

Logan rubbed his forehead and drew in a deep breath. His son was as subtle as a bombing raid.

Krista pushed her chair back. "I really have to go home. The cats are waiting for their dinner."

"Daddy will walk you home," Lauren said firmly.

Krista looked at Logan, her lips twitching. "Haven't we done this scene before?"

"This is Take Two." They both stood, and he took her arm. "See you later, kids."

"Much later," Mitch said, chortling gleefully.

Logan decided as he and Krista walked the two blocks to her house that he may as well bring the subject out in the open. "I feel I ought to apologize for my children's Machiavellian matchmaking." If he knew his kids—and he did—they wouldn't let up, and the potential for awkwardness and unease was staggering. "I hope you weren't embarrassed."

"No." Krista smiled, relieved that Logan had said something. She knew *he'd* been embarrassed. The expression on his face had given him away. She decided to make light of the whole thing. "I wonder if we're about to be subjected to an Amy Sue campaign in reverse?"

Logan's smile was definitely forced, Krista thought. Obviously he didn't like to joke about his sweet, traditional girlfriend. Too bad he was the only one who didn't know the woman was a piranha in disguise! They walked to her front door and she fumbled in her purse for her key.

"I want to congratulate you on your victory in the Marshall case," Logan said, watching her. "Your research, your presentation—everything was suberb in every way. It was one of the easiest judgments I've ever had to make."

Krista's smile was glowing. "Thank you, Logan."

"And I agreed completely with your dissertation on the plight of the displaced homemaker. It's a very depressing scenario—a woman is married for years, takes care of her husband and the house, raises the children, and is suddenly cast out when her husband decides to sample the charms of a younger woman. Having never worked, she has no job skills to support herself and often faces true poverty for the first time in her life. I'm glad Alice Marshall found an attorney to represent her so skillfully."

"And I'm glad you ruled in her favor," said Krista. "And that Wilson Marshall decided to skimp on his attorney's fee and went for Fleener rather than someone like Ross Perry."

"Fleener was atrocious," Logan agreed. "But I tend to favor the displaced homemaker despite the competency of her attorney. Unlike you, counselor, I don't care to sit on both sides of the fence in moral issues."

The edge in his tone was unmistakable. Krista stared at him. "What do you mean?"

"I mean that you represent whoever happens to be your client, regardless of your personal beliefs. If Wilson Marshall had asked you to represent him, you would've done everything in your power to keep Alice from winning the kind of settlement she won today."

"That's not true!" Krista said hotly.

"Isn't it?"

"No! I would never encourage a client of mine to try to cheat his spouse out of what is legally hers!"

"You're an honorable barracuda, then?" Logan took

her key ring from her and inserted one of the keys into the lock. Maddeningly enough, it proved to be the correct key. He opened the door, fastened an arm around her waist, and swept her inside into the small, dark foyer. "Honey, 'honorable barracuda' is an oxymoron. A complete contradiction in terms."

She jerked away from him. "You can make judgments in the courtroom, Your Honor, but you have no right to pass moral judgment on me!" She glowered at him, her chest heaving with indignation. "Your—your unmitigated gall takes my breath away!"

Logan's feelings for Krista had been building and building, and suddenly they exploded as he stared down into her hot blue eyes. "*This* takes your breath away," he said, and hauled her into his arms before she had time to blink. Instinctively, Krista splayed her fingers against his chest. Then his mouth, hard and commanding, took possession of hers.

She reacted automatically to the display of masculine aggression. Though her hands were trapped between them, she managed to work one free to push at his shoulder in an attempt to free herself. Her efforts were futile. He was so big, so strong. He surrounded her completely, his hold too powerful to break.

After just a few moments, though, she didn't want to be free. His mouth was moving over hers, hot and firm and demanding. His tongue thrust between her lips and her mouth opened wider for him. She tasted him; she inhaled his heady masculine scent. She felt the hard warmth of his body pressing against her as his tongue penetrated her mouth, full and deep, in an incredibly arousing erotic simulation of lovemaking.

Her eyes closed heavily and her hand stopped pushing against his shoulder. It instead curled around his neck in an age-old gesture of surrender. The carefully hidden but powerful romantic streak in her character rose swiftly to the fore. It had finally happened to her! she thought dizzily. She'd finally met the man who could sweep her off her feet.

Everything made sense to her now, from her intense awareness of Logan the moment she'd laid eyes on him in the courtroom, to her unusually impassioned responses to him. Even his immediate antagonism toward her seemed logical now. He had experienced the same strong feelings for her and had been knocked as off balance as she. But beneath his facade of hostility, of disapproval, he had been drawn to her. He'd wanted her—as he wanted her now.

The kiss went on and on, deepening, growing wilder, hotter. Logan's hands slipped into the back pockets of her jeans and he cupped her firm buttocks, kneading with his long fingers and lifting her against him.

She moaned into his mouth. The evidence of his passion was hard and thick between them. "Logan." She wasn't sure if she spoke his name aloud or if it was reverberating inside her head. She twisted in his arms, trying to get closer, to have more of him.

She'd never felt this way before. She'd never experienced such a profound and elemental need to merge with a man, to claim him as her own as surely as he had branded her as his. Her body was aching, throbbing, burning. For Logan. Only for Logan.

He lifted her, holding her high against his chest. Her arms encircled his neck and her fingers stroked his nape, gently tangling in his thick dark hair.

They were halfway up the stairs when a bundle of fur and claws came flying through the air, seemingly out of nowhere, and landed directly on Krista's stomach. Krista was too caught up in the throes of passion to react sensibly and rationally. Had she been in full command of her faculties, she might have immediately realized that it was Tao who had launched himself like a missile from the top step in a typical bid for attention.

But her Siamese cat was the last thing on her mind as Logan romantically carried her up the stairs, and Tao's unexpected landing caught her completely unawares. She screamed and jerked wildly, causing the skitterish cat to beat a frantic retreat onto Logan's shoulder, his claws digging in with needlelike sharpness.

"Good Lord!" Logan yelled. "What is it?" Things were happening too fast for his passion-drugged mind to assimilate. He dropped Krista as he tried frantically to free himself from the furry mass clinging to his shoulder. Tao meowed loudly and hung on.

"A cat?" Logan's brain finally began to function. He'd been attacked by a cat, which had fastened itself onto his shoulder and refused to be dislodged.

Had he been watching the scene, he probably would have found it funny. Living it, however, placed a great strain on his sense of humor. "What the hell is going on, Krista?"

Krista had returned to earth with a jarring thud, accelerated by her landing on the carpeted steps on her knees. She quickly got to her feet and went downstairs to grope in the darkness for the light switch at the foot of the stairs. When the lights came on, Logan found himself staring into the deep blue eyes of an outraged Siamese cat.

He made a grab for the cat. Tao meowed indignantly and jumped down, one back claw leaving in its wake a long scratch on Logan's neck.

Krista's eyes widened at the sight of blood. "Logan, I'm so sorry!" She dashed up the stairs to his side. "Oh, he really tore the skin! Let me—"

Logan backed down a step. "What else do you have lurking around here besides killer felines? Homicidal police dogs? Man-eating Dobermans?"

"I just have the two cats and—"

"There's *two* of them? When does the other one strike?"

"Logan, this has never happened before. Tao is usually very gentle. He—he wanted attention, and he thinks he's still a kitten. You see, he always used to jump on shoulders when he was little and—"

"His claws hadn't grown into daggers yet," Logan finished wryly. He gingerly touched the scratch with his fingers, and his eyes met Krista's.

"Let me clean that scratch for you," she said huskily. "I'll wash it off and put an astringent on it." She caught his hand in hers and gave a tug. "Come on."

Logan allowed her to lead him into the green and ivory bathroom, where he sat down on the wide edge of the forest-green tub. "So the counselor dabbles in medicine as a sideline, hmm?" His gaze swept over her, taking in the sight of her trembling hands, the uneven rising and falling of her breasts. She was all shook up, as the old song went. And not because of the cat, he was certain of that.

A rush of pure masculine triumph surged through him. *He* was the one who had shattered Krista Conway's composure. His prowess had turned the lady bomber into a woman quivering with passion for him. *For him!*

He forgot the cat and the scratch. An unholy delight filled him, and he put his hands on her hips and pulled her between his legs. Krista's heart thumped, and her hand shook as she dabbed a soapy washcloth along the length of the scratch. "This—this will just take a minute," she said, trying to cover her awkwardness. "I hope it doesn't hurt too much."

"Oh, I'm hurting like hell." Logan smiled a hungry crocodile's smile. He felt bold and aggressive, the swaggering, conquering male. "But not where you're touching me. It hurts where you're *not* touching me."

He watched her blue eyes widen, saw the pink flush stain her cheeks. It was thrilling to discover he possessed this potent sexual power over her. He'd been strict and conservative and judicious, the model citizen and parent, for such a long time, he was unaware there could be other dimensions to his personality.

Krista tried to distract herself from Logan's innuendos with the task at hand. She poured some hydrogen peroxide on a cotton ball and touched it to his scratch. "I know this must sting," she said lightly, striving to diffuse the sexually charged atmosphere. "You're very brave not to holler ouch."

"Do I get a reward for being so brave?" Her breasts were on a level with his face. His senses were swimming. "I know what I'd like." His hold on her tightened, anchoring her firmly in place, and his mouth opened boldly over one cloth-covered breast. Even through the double barrier of her bra and blouse, he could feel the softness of the breast and hardness of her nipple.

"Logan!" Krista gasped. Her knees nearly buckled, and she clutched at his shoulders. His mouth moved over her, and she drew in a sharp breath as a shaft of arousal pierced her very core.

"I want to see you," he said. His onyx eyes were glazed. "I want to touch you and taste you. I want to make love to you." His fingers impatiently sought the buttons of her blouse. "Now, Krista. Let's go to bed."

She wanted to yield to him. The romantic in her yearned for completion with this special man who'd awakened her to a passion she'd never dreamed she was capable of. But her instincts were so closely attuned to Logan that she picked up something in his tone besides the passion and urgency that had commanded her evocative response earlier. There was a certain kind of hard male insistence—she couldn't have put it into words if she'd tried—that put her instinctively on guard.

"Logan," she said softly, "it's too soon." Her head

was beginning to clear, and she attempted to explain her feelings to him. "I didn't mean to lead you on, to start something I didn't intend to finish. My behavior tonight has been totally out of character for me. I don't know what came over me. I don't indulge in casual affairs. I've never gone to bed with a man I've only known a few days."

"You haven't?"

He sounded patently disbelieving, and her stomach tightened. "No, I haven't." She felt hot all over, as if she were burning with fever. The truth was dawning, and it hurt. "But you think I do this sort of thing all the time, don't you? Meet a man, take him to bed with me . . ."

She could see it in his eyes, and a great wave of anger washed over her. An anger that was mixed equally with disappointment and pain. Her passionate response to Logan had been unique for her, something special, something evoked by the magical chemistry between them. She'd thought it had been the same for him. And she'd been wrong, so wrong.

"You think I'm one of those hedonistic swingers," she said, "who blithely jumps in and out of bed with whoever happens to come along, and—and you thought you'd grab a piece of the action yourself." Her voice rose. What a fool she'd made of herself! What an even bigger fool she'd nearly been! "This all has been just a sexual ego trip for you!"

Logan stood up. He towered over her, but she wasn't intimidated by his superior height. "I wanted to make love to you tonight," he said thickly. The hurt in her blue eyes ripped at him. He felt like a cad, an unscrupulous user. The feeling was new to him, and he hated it.

"You wanted it, too, Krista," he went on. "Don't try to tell me you didn't." He knew he was attempting to assuage his guilt. She was a slick city sophisticate, that "*Cosmo* girl." Weren't such women supposed to take things like seduction and one-night stands in stride?

Krista stormed out of the bathroom and down the stairs. Logan swiftly followed her. "Get out of my house!" she ordered, and opened the front door to further clarify her point.

He stared at her. Her eyes were bright. With un-shed tears? He was horrified. He'd never made a woman cry. "Krista, I—"

"I want you to get out!"

"I'm sorry that—"

"You're only sorry that you didn't score tonight." She should have guessed, should have known, Krista thought scornfully. His attitudes toward women were out of the Stone Age, and she'd been stupid enough to let herself be swept off her feet. She'd been fool-ishly naïve and pathetically romantic. She'd been everything she normally was not.

She sank her teeth into her lower lip and shrugged. Her anger was fading, and she now felt weary and depressed. "I suppose I can't blame you," she said flatly. "We were operating on different wavelengths, that's all. You thought you were hopping into the sack with a sexually liberated free spirit. You thought I view sex as a lark."

Wouldn't he be amazed, she thought, to learn that her feelings about sex and love were probably more old-fashioned and traditional than that living Barbie doll Amy Sue's? He wouldn't believe it. Not Logan Moore, the man who fit women into neat categories: virgins, however scheming, deserved respect and mar-riage, while successful professional women were to be used for meaningless sex.

Logan saw the flash of disillusionment that shad-owed her sapphire eyes. It was infinitely worse than her anger. He'd hurt her, he thought bleakly. She was different from any woman he'd ever met. He'd never imagined that a woman like her would want him, but she had. And he'd hurt her. Oh, yes, there were dimensions to his personality he'd never dreamed existed. Alarming ones.

"Good night, Logan," she said pointedly. She wouldn't look at him.

"We were operating on different wavelengths," he repeated thoughtfully. "If I thought I was trysting with a sexually free spirit, what were you thinking, Krista?"

Oh, if he only knew . . . Krista's face burned. He thought she was a seasoned veteran of the sexual revolution; he would never believe she'd romantically fantasized him as her lover destined by fate. Now that she was out of his arms and released from the grip of passion, she could hardly believe it herself.

"Krista?" Logan took a step closer.

She moved away. "Just go home, Logan," she said wearily.

Tao chose that moment to join them, winding around their ankles and purring loudly in a blatant bid for attention. "*Now* he wants to be friends," Logan said wryly. He stooped down to pet the cat at the same time that Krista bent to pick him up. Their hands touched over Tao's sleek fur. Their faces were very close.

"Krista," Logan said tentatively. He ached for her. She'd been so soft and sweet, so pliant and responsive in his arms. And he'd blown it by trying to play superstud. He'd been caught up in his own role and had tried to take selfishly what she had generously wanted to give him.

She stood up, the cat in her arms. "Good-bye, Logan," she said with unmistakable finality.

He knew it would be foolish to press her. He'd already done everything else wrong tonight; it was definitely time to leave. "Good night, Krista," he said quietly, and walked out of the house. She quickly closed the front door behind him.

For a long moment, each stood on opposite sides of the closed door, staring at it. Then Tao jumped down from Krista's arms and ran toward the kitchen, meowing insistently, demanding that she follow him. She did.

Outside, Logan cast a final glance at the heavy door and began to walk slowly up the street toward his home.

Six

Lauren was sitting on the front porch step when Krista pulled into her driveway the next afternoon. Ink, the big black tomcat, was snoozing peacefully in the little girl's arms.

"Hi, Krissy!" Lauren called. "I found Ink on the porch. And guess what? He's been hunting again. There was a dead chipmunk in the yard."

"Oh, no!" Krista groaned and made a face. Ink was forever depositing his victims in the yard. And there were many; he was something akin to a contract killer in the cat world. "The devil dashed out the door as I was on my way to the office this morning. Naturally, he ran when I tried to catch him, and I had to leave for an appointment." Krista patted the cat's big head. He opened one yellow eye and surveyed her with an air of boredom. Lauren grinned up at her.

Krista smiled back. She was relieved to see Lauren today. Driving home from the office this afternoon, she'd wondered if last night's debacle with Logan would mean an end to her friendship with his daughter. The thought had depressed her. She was genuinely fond of Lauren and looked forward to her daily visits.

"I buried the chipmunk in the petunias," Lauren said as she trotted inside after Krista, the big cat in her arms. "I used a rock to dig."

"Thank you, Lauren. It's a relief not to have to face digging a grave after a long day at the office."

Obviously, Krista thought with relief, the child had no idea what had transpired between her and her father last night. She and Lauren could continue their friendship without the haunting specter of Logan between them.

Tao greeted them in the hall with a raucous meow. "Want me to feed them?" Lauren asked, putting down Ink to pick up Tao.

"That would be wonderful, honey. It'll give me a chance to go upstairs and change." Krista gave the child a grateful smile and headed up the stairs. Lauren knew where everything was in the kitchen, and Krista took the opportunity to slip out of her burgundy and gray silk dress and into a pair of slim royal-blue cotton slacks and a cotton blouse splashed with a bright comic-book print.

She caught sight of her reflection in the closet mirror as she hung up her dress. There were circles under her eyes and her face was pale and drawn. Today had been a particularly trying day. Marcia Landau had been in, alternately weeping and cursing about the upcoming custody fight between her and her husband. "I'll give up every penny of my settlement, but I have to have sole custody of little Julie!" Marcia had cried over and over again. It seemed to have become an obsession with the woman.

From what Krista had learned from Ross Perry, Gary Landau held the same sentiments. "I'll give Marcia everything I own, she can have *everything*, but I have to have sole custody of little Julie!" was Gary Landau's passionate refrain. Custody cases were always emotional and difficult for all concerned, but the Landau case promised to be exceptionally so.

Krista sighed as she started down the stairs. She knew she couldn't blame her low spirits solely on the Landau case. She looked tired today because she *was* tired. She'd lain awake for hours last night reliving those tempestuous moments in Logan Moore's arms. And she'd flinched every time she came to the last part, the part when she'd realized that Logan saw her only as a hot number in the sack. She was nothing more to him than a sexual boost to his male ego while she . . .

She shook her head as if to clear it of the disturbing memories. She'd reacted to Logan Moore like a dewy-eyed romantic. Not to mention an addle-brained one. She'd gotten exactly what she deserved.

Her gaze fell automatically on the calendar as she walked into the kitchen. It was the twenty-fifth of September.

Six years ago on this date, her brother Eric and Eric's law partner, Craig Raddison, had been killed when the private plane they'd been aboard had crashed in the mountains of western Virginia. Krista had driven them to the airport, and the picture of Eric, tall and blond, as he strode toward the small twin-engine plane flashed before her mind's eye. It was odd that she could remember every nuance, every detail about Eric when she had trouble conjuring up any kind of image of Craig. Odd because she'd been engaged to Craig Raddison. They'd planned to be married within the next year.

The phone began to ring, disrupting her sad musings. Lauren jumped to answer it, and Krista had to smile. The little girl's eager enthusiasm to answer the phone never failed to amuse her.

It was Krista's aunt Helen on the line. "I've been thinking of you all day today, Krista. I couldn't let this date pass without calling you."

There were other calls after that. Two from old college chums, three from the close friends who'd been with her the day she'd heard the terrible news. Her parents. A cousin. Another aunt.

"You sure do get a lot of phone calls," Lauren said when Krista finished with another call. "How come everybody is calling to talk about Eric?"

Lauren had been sitting at the kitchen table, drawing with the pad and colored markers that Krista kept on hand for her. Obviously, she'd been listening in on the telephone conversations going on around her.

"Today is a special kind of anniversary in my family, Lauren," Krista explained. "A sad one. My brother Eric was killed in a plane crash six years ago today."

Lauren got up and put her arms around Krista, hugging her tight. Krista's arms automatically encircled the firm little body, and she held Lauren close. She was deeply touched. She hadn't expected an empathetic response from a child, but then Lauren was a child who'd been touched by tragedy and loss herself, with her mother's death four years ago.

There was something inherently comforting in holding the little girl, Krista thought. Children were a source of hope and joy, a continuity linking the past with the present and the future. Unexpectedly, Logan came to her mind. She decided he must derive great comfort in having three children who lived as a testament to the love he and his wife had shared.

If only Eric had had a child, she thought, sighing softly. But he'd assumed there would be plenty of time for that. He hadn't been in any hurry to settle down and marry; he was having too much fun playing the field.

But Eric was a part of *her*, wasn't he? There was no reason why he couldn't live on through a child of hers. The thought was a source of both comfort and pain, for there was certainly no child of her own within the foreseeable future.

The brass knocker on the front door sounded once with a brief staccato rap, then the doorbell rang.

Lauren looked up at Krista, and they smiled at each other. They walked together to the door, Lauren's arm securely wrapped around Krista's waist and Krista's arm around the little girl's shoulders.

Logan stood on the small porch. "Hi, Daddy!" Lauren flung herself into his arms. Logan's eyes met and held Krista's above the child's head.

Krista felt her stomach do a triple somersault. She quickly looked away, not caring that she was the first to break the gaze. She wasn't ready to see Logan again. Her heart began to thud against her ribs. Why did he have to come for Lauren today, of all days? In the past, Denise or Mitch had always phoned or come for Lauren themselves.

"Denise and Mitch are in the car," Logan said. "We're on our way to that seafood restaurant on the highway. Would you like to join us for dinner, Krista?"

"Oh, yes, Krissy! Please say yes!" Lauren cried, jumping up and down.

She would have liked to say yes, to please Lauren, but there was no way she was going to subject herself to the pain and embarrassment of Logan Moore's company. "I'm sorry, but I really can't," she said. She turned to go back inside.

Logan was suddenly close behind her, so close that she could feel his warm breath fan the nape of her neck. "We all would like you to come with us, Krista."

"No!" She was protesting her instantaneous sensual response to him as much as his words. He held a powerful sexual magnetism for her, and last night's unhappy episode hadn't seemed to diminish it in the slightest.

A flash of impatience surged through Logan. He was accustomed to being obeyed, due to his judicial position and the strength of his own personality. The urge to brush aside Krista's refusal and simply snatch her up and carry her to the car held an incredible appeal.

He forced the urge aside. "Please come, Krista," he said instead, his voice deep. He'd spent half of last night and most of today thinking about her—and chastising himself for so totally misjudging her.

She hadn't responded to him merely because he was a willing male and she, the liberated female, wanted to add another figurative notch to her figurative bedpost. He had taken the special passion that had flared between them and used it against her. He'd hurt her, and by the rigidity of her posture and the chill in her blue eyes, she was not going to give him another chance.

"Don't you like fish, Krissy?" Lauren asked. "We could go somewhere else, couldn't we, Daddy?"

Krista suppressed a groan. "Lauren, I do like fish, but—"

"Don't you want to have dinner with us?" Lauren gazed from Krista to her father, a stricken look in her big brown eyes.

"Of course I'd like to have dinner with you," Krista said. "It's just that I have some papers to look over tonight, and . . ." Her gaze flicked over Lauren's worried face. She didn't want to hurt the little girl's feelings. And hadn't she decided that her friendship with the Moore children would stand independent of her dealings with their father? "But I guess I ought to take time out to eat, hmm?"

"Yes!" Lauren looked relieved. She caught Krista's hand, then took her father's hand, too. "C'mon, let's go!" She tried to pull the two forward.

Krista laughed at her determination. "I need a minute to get my purse and run a comb through my hair."

"No need to bother with the comb," Logan said quietly. "You look beautiful as always, counselor."

She gave him a frigid look and refrained from comment.

Mitch and Denise greeted her warmly as she approached the Moores' car, a mud-brown Dodge Aries.

"You can sit in the back with me and Denise, Krissy," Lauren said happily.

"I think Mitch will give up the front seat to our guest," Logan interjected quickly.

Mitch groaned. "Dad, I hardly fit in the backseat." He gave Krista a martyred look. "Did you know this car is one of the ten least-stolen cars in America? I can list the reasons why."

"Mitch is hoping you'll offer to drive your car, Krista," Denise said, grinning. "He's in love with your Bentley. He's been dying for a ride in it."

Mitch didn't bother to deny it. "Your car is the most terrific car I've ever seen. I mean it, Krista, it's totally out of hand."

"I remember my brother at sixteen," Krista said, and smiled in reminiscence. "He was car-mad!" If Eric had been given the chance to drive a sapphire-blue Bentley convertible at sixteen, he would've thought he'd attained nirvana. Her smile broadened. "Would you like to drive my car to the restaurant, Mitch?"

"*Would* I?" Mitch looked stunned. "*Could* I?"

"Absolutely not," said his father.

Krista dug into her purse and handed Mitch the car keys. "I assume you have a driver's license?"

"I've had it for four months!" Mitch took the keys, his dark eyes alight.

"Krista, I don't think it's a good idea," Logan said.

"Why not? He's a licensed driver and the restaurant's only a ten-minute drive from here." Krista's voice was challenging. "I assure you that my insurance is fully paid, Judge Moore."

"Let him drive, Daddy," Lauren said.

"We've got nothing to lose but our lives," Denise added cheekily.

"Denise!" Logan frowned at her flippancy. "Mitchell, you— "

No one but Krista was there to listen to him. Mitch, Denise, and Lauren were already piling into the Bentley, parked in Krista's driveway. "You lost this round, Your Honor," Krista said. She tossed him a cold little smile and walked off to join the others.

Mitch drove to the restaurant without incident. He was actually an extremely cautious driver, Krista noted with amusement. He stopped for a full two or three minutes at every stop sign whether there was any oncoming traffic or not. Krista sat in the front seat beside him and Logan rode in the back with Denise and Lauren.

They had a good time at the restaurant. The food was excellent, and by conversing with and through the children, neither Logan nor Krista felt the awkwardness they had anticipated. Logan insisted on driving back, and Krista hid a secret smile. Apparently Mitch wasn't the only one who'd been admiring the Bentley and nurturing a desire to drive it.

Krista didn't give it a thought when Logan pulled the car up in front of his house, assuming he and the children would get out here and she would drive herself home. Logan had other ideas.

"You three go on in, and I'll take Krista home," he told the children.

"There's no need," Krista said from the backseat where she was sitting with the girls. "I'm perfectly capable of driving myself home."

"Of course you are," Logan said heartily. "But I intend to see you safely to your door."

Krista wanted to tell him that if last night were any indication, she'd be a lot safer going home alone. But Mitch, Denise, and Lauren were very much present, and she didn't dare mention last night with the three of them around.

"A gentleman always sees a lady to her door." Logan imparted this platitude to Mitch.

"But suppose the lady in question doesn't want the gentleman to see her to her door?" Krista asked.

Logan surveyed her lazily. "The gentleman sees the lady to her door, anyway."

"That attitude is more chauvinistic than chivalrous, Your Honor. Let's get out, kids."

She and the three children quickly climbed out of the car. Logan remained seated behind the wheel. He seemed to have no intention of moving.

"Here's the housekey," he said. He removed a key from his key chain and handed it to Mitch. "I'll be back just as soon as I drive Krista home. I have to pick up our car at her place, too." His bland smile set Krista's teeth on edge.

He had her there, she fumed to herself. And he knew it. She had no choice but to allow him to drive her to her house so he could reclaim his car. She said good night to the kids and got into the front seat. Logan waited until the three children were inside the house, then pulled away from the curb.

Neither spoke a word during the short ride. The moment he stopped in front of her house, Krista reached for the door handle.

"Wait!" Logan leaned across the seat and caught her arm, restraining her. "I'll come around and open the door for you."

"A gentleman always opens a door for a lady? The kids aren't here, Logan. You don't have to go through the motions of etiquette on my behalf."

He didn't release her arm. "I want to, Krista."

"Why? You don't think I'm a lady. Last night you made it quite clear what you thought I was." She instantly regretted the words. The last thing she wanted to discuss with him was last night!

"I think you're very much a lady and I want to prove to you that I can be a gentleman. I want to talk to you about last night, Krista." His grip remained firm, but his fingers began to caress her upper arm lightly, almost absently. "I want to tell you how sorry I am for hurting you. Would it help to know how deeply I regret it?"

Her heart lurched. She was intensely aware of his nearness, of the strength of his hard frame as he held her. If she were to lean back just a few inches, her head would be resting against his broad shoulder. Her desire to do just that alarmed her.

"Krista." His voice was husky, sexily so.

She felt a panicky urge to run away from him, and immediately quashed it. She couldn't allow herself to behave like a jittery Victorian maiden. She wouldn't let him reduce her to that! "Last night was a mistake for both of us, Judge Moore." She firmly and purposefully removed his hand from her arm. "I suggest we both forget it."

"I agree. Let's put it behind us . . . and start over again. Will you have dinner with me tomorrow night?"

"No, thank you. I have other plans."

He frowned. "A date?"

"Yes. We man-eaters have to devour our quota of fresh meat, you know." She shoved open the door and got out of the car.

With growing frustration, Logan watched her leave. She was making it extremely clear that she didn't want to have anything more to do with him. And he had no idea how to change her mind, he realized bleakly.

Reluctantly, he climbed out of the car and handed her her keys. She strode briskly to her front door, and he followed, a pace or two behind.

The moment Krista saw the door standing slightly ajar, she knew something was wrong. She'd pulled the door shut and locked it when she had left with Lauren and Logan, she was certain of that. And there was something else not right, something she hadn't noticed until now. The house was completely dark. She knew she'd left on the hall light.

She turned in sudden confusion and crashed into Logan, standing directly in back of her. His hands automatically closed over her shoulders to steady her.

"Logan, I locked the door before I left." Her mouth felt dry, and the boulder of apprehension that had lodged in her throat made it difficult to swallow. "And—and I know I left the hall light on."

Logan stared at the door and the total darkness within. His brows pulled together in concern. "It looks like someone's broken in."

Her heart seemed to stop, then to start up again at a wild pace. "I—I didn't want to hear that," she said nervously, moistening her lips with her tongue. She'd wanted him to deny what she was fearing. "I was counting on you to say something patronizing like, 'Are you sure you locked the door? Are you sure you left the light on?' "

"Krista, I saw you switch on the light and I watched you lock the door."

Her gaze flew to his face. "Th-then you think—" She couldn't finish.

"Let's go next door to the neighbors' and ask to use their phone to call the police." His arm slid around her shoulder, and he turned her away from the door to guide her down the walk.

Suddenly, they heard a meow. "Tao!" Krista tore away from Logan and pushed the door open wide. "If they hurt him . . ."

"Krista, don't go in," Logan said. "The burglars could still be in there and—" He broke off when he realized Krista wasn't going to listen to him. She was already inside.

He followed her in. She had flicked on the lights and was cuddling the purring Siamese cat in her arms. "He seems to be all right," she whispered shakily, petting him.

Logan strode swiftly into the living room and switched on a lamp. The room was in complete disarray with tables and chairs and lamps overturned.

A flash of black fur streaked from behind the sofa into the hall.

"Ink is okay, too," Krista said with relief as she joined Logan in the living room. "Oh!" She gasped at the sight.

"Do you know what's missing?" Logan asked tersely.

She nodded. "The television set. The VCR and the stereo. The room is such a wreck I can't tell if anything else is gone." She was trembling. She'd never been robbed before. The sight of the ransacked room, the thought of a stranger breaking into her house and rummaging through her things, taking her property, made her feel sick.

She swallowed back the bile that burned her throat and clutched the cat closer. Tao objected to the tightness of her grip. With an indignant meow, he wriggled free and jumped from her arms to charge up the staircase. She turned to follow him.

"Krista, don't go up. If—"

Once again, she didn't listen. She raced up the stairs, calling Tao.

There were no burglars in the house, but they'd made their presence felt. Drawers were pulled out and overturned in the upstairs room that Krista had set up as an office. Papers were everywhere. In the three bedrooms, her own and the two guest rooms, drawers had been emptied, and clothing and towels and bed linens were strewn all over the floor.

"There was a small portable TV up here and it's gone," Krista said. She stared at the disorder that earlier had been her neat and well-kept bedroom. "And my jewelry box is missing."

Logan stared closely at Krista. She was pale and trembling. "Sit down," he ordered, and guided her to the bed. He gently pushed her to sit on the edge of it. "I'm going to call the police."

Everything felt unreal to Krista, as if she were in a dream. She listened to Logan dial the 911 emergency number, identify himself, and give the address. After completing the call, he sat down beside her and took her hand in his. "They said they'll be here soon. Just sit here and try to relax, Krista."

"Thank you for staying with me, Logan. I—I would've hated to have faced this by myself." Her voice sounded as if it were coming from someone else. She hung onto Logan's hand, needing the strength and warmth it imparted. She was shaking, her insides were churning, and she was inordinately grateful for his calm presence.

He put his arms around her and she buried her face against his chest. He held her tightly, and she felt incredibly protected. They sat in silence until the police arrived. Krista's legs felt weak and rubbery as she and Logan started down the stairs. She held tightly to the bannister.

Logan put his arm around her waist. "Easy, now," he said softly. She allowed herself to lean against him and gave him a small, grateful smile that touched his heart.

"The contents of your jewelry box?" prompted the officer. He and his partner had checked through the house and he was now writing a list of the missing articles.

"There wasn't too much in it," Krista said. She tried to remember. "I'm wearing my watch." And her grandmother's opal ring and Eric's gold signet ring. They were sentimentally irreplaceable and she was thankful they hadn't been lost to her. "I had some good costume jewelry and— Oh, no! My engagement ring!" She gasped at the realization.

"Diamond?" the policeman asked. "How many carats?"

"Three," she said softly.

The police officer whistled through his teeth at the size of the gem and went back to his paperwork.

Logan gaped at her, his head reeling—and not from the size of the diamond. "Your engagement ring?" he asked. It was suddenly difficult to breathe. "*You're engaged*?"

"I was engaged," she corrected him. "Craig was killed in a plane crash six years ago today, along with my brother Eric."

"Eric is dead?" Logan stared at her, his shock at Eric's death superseding the shock of Krista's engagement ring. He took both her hands in his. "Krista, I'm so sorry. From everything you've told me about Eric, I'd begun to feel a certain kinship with him."

And from the fond and frequent allusions Krista made to her brother, Logan could guess how greatly she suffered his loss. "I know what it's like to lose someone you love deeply," he went on. "And to lose both your brother and your fiancé at the same time must have been devastating."

Krista saw the compassion and understanding in Logan's warm ebony eyes. "Yes," she said quietly. "It was a terrible loss." She held on to his hands, basking in the solace of his gaze. She felt a bond between them, two people who had survived tragedy and rebuilt their lives, who were sadder and wiser and stronger as well.

The policeman rejoined them. "I'll file this report. But don't count on getting anything back, even if we catch the thieves," he added discouragingly. "They usually get rid of the stuff right after they take it."

"Do you have any suspects in mind? Any idea of who did it?" Logan asked.

The policeman shook his head. "There's been a rash of burglaries around here. We think it's juveniles needing quick cash for drugs. The same type of stuff is taken from all the houses, TV's and things like that. Stuff they can sell quickly on the street. They've passed up valuable paintings and expensive art collections because they obviously don't know their worth." He frowned at the broken lock on the front door. "I suggest you get good deadbolt locks for all your doors, Miss Conway. This particular type of lock is useless. Any amateur can break in with it, as we've seen."

The police officers left, and Logan and Krista faced each other in the hallway. "I hardly know where to begin the cleanup," Krista said. "I'd finally gotten everything put away from the move and now I have to start all over again." Her voice was shaky, and she tried to smile.

"You're not going to do anything tonight," Logan said firmly. "I'm taking you home to spend the night at our house."

She should refuse, Krista told herself. There was so much to be done here, she should start working on it right away. "It's kind of you to offer, but I'll be all right here, Logan."

"Go upstairs and pack a bag, Krista."

"I'm not afraid to stay alone. I—"

"Or I'll pack it for you. Your clothes should be easy enough to find. They're all over the floor."

"I can't leave the cats here alone." She guessed she must sound irrational. She'd left the cats overnight before. But at the moment she was feeling somewhat irrational.

"We'll take them with us. I'll load their paraphernalia into my car while you're packing."

"Logan, what if they—the burglars—what if they come back?" She didn't want to be afraid to stay in her own house, but despite her brave words, she didn't want to be here tonight.

"They won't be back," he promised. "They've already taken what they wanted from here." He took her hand and led her up the steps. "Get your things together, Krista."

She obeyed like someone in a trance, going through the motions of packing without being fully aware of what she was doing. Logan loaded her bag and the cats and the cat box and cat dishes and cat food into his car while she sat in the front seat, feeling dazed.

She must be in shock, Krista mused hazily. It was a relief to let Logan do the thinking, to make the decisions. Once again she was profoundly grateful for his presence.

Mitch, Denise, and Lauren were upset by the news of the burglary, although Lauren's delight in having the cats at her house somewhat tempered her outrage. Mitch carried Krista's bag into one of the extra bedrooms and pointed out the adjoining bath. Denise brought her a stack of magazines. Lauren asked to have both cats sleep in her room. Then Logan evicted all three kids from Krista's bedroom.

"Krista's had a rough time tonight," she heard him explain firmly as he ushered them into the hall. "She needs peace and quiet."

She actually was sorry to see them leave. She tried to interest herself in one of the magazines Denise had given her, but to no avail. She felt jittery and tense. When it suddenly thundered, she started. The bright flash of lightning in the sky further unnerved her.

She took a long bath, hoping it would relax her, and changed into her nightgown, a silky slip-style one in a pastel blue. The noise of the rain pounding against the windowpane made her jump. She sighed. The bath hadn't helped. She was still wound tight as a spring.

Knowing it was useless, she nevertheless climbed into bed to try to sleep. An hour later, she switched on the bedside lamp and reached for one of Denise's magazines. The rain hadn't abated, and bolts of lightning periodically lit up the sky. The claps of thunder seemed to be getting louder. The printed words on the page blurred

She thought of Logan. What if he hadn't insisted on seeing her to her door tonight? She would have had to face the nightmare of the burglary all on her own. She remembered the feel of his big hand clasping hers, of his steadying arm around her.

He had been so kind, so supportive. Had she told him how much she appreciated all his help? Had she thanked him for everything he'd done for her tonight? He'd comforted her and dealt with the police. He'd made four trips to the car with the cats and all their equipment, he'd uncomplainingly changed the litter in the cat box before stashing it on the floor of the backseat of his car!

She really had to thank him properly, Krista decided. She padded across the room and was about to pull her pink velour robe from her suitcase when there was a slight tap at the door.

Before she could move or speak, the door opened and Logan walked into the room.

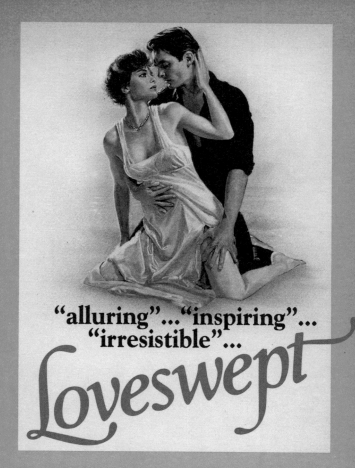

"alluring"... "inspiring"...
"irresistible"...

Loveswept

America's most popular, most compelling romance novels...

Loveswept

Here, at last...love stories that really involve you! Fresh, finely crafted novels with story lines so believable you'll feel you're actually living them!

Read a Loveswept novel and you'll experience all the very real feelings of two people as they discover and build an involved relationship: laughing, crying, learning and loving. Characters you can relate to... exciting places to visit...unexpected plot twists...all in all, exciting romances that satisfy your mind and delight your heart.

And now you can be sure you'll never, ever miss a single Loveswept title by enrolling in our special reader's home delivery service. A service that will bring all four new Loveswept romances published every month into your home—and deliver them to you *before* they appear in the bookstores!

Examine 4 Loveswept Novels for

15 Days FREE!

To introduce you to this fabulous service, you'll get four brand-new Loveswept releases not yet in the bookstores. These four exciting new titles are yours to examine for 15 days without obligation to buy. Keep them if you wish for just $9.95 plus postage and handling and any applicable sales tax.

SEND NO MONEY NOW.
RETURN THIS
POSTAGE-PAID CARD TODAY!

FREE TRIAL/HOME DELIVERY ORDER CARD

Loveswept
Bantam Books, P.O. Box 985, Hicksville, NY 11802

☐ Please send me four new romances for a 15-day FREE examination.
If I keep them, I will pay just $9.95 plus postage and handling and any
applicable sales tax and you will enter my name on your preferred cus-
tomer list to receive all four new Loveswept novels published each month
before they are released to the bookstores—always on the same 15-day
free examination basis.   20123

Name_____

Address_____

City_____

State_____Zip_____

My Guarantee: I am never required to buy any shipment unless I wish. I
may preview each shipment for 15 days. If I don't want it, I simply return the
shipment within 15 days and owe nothing for it.   N1

Seven

They stared at each other for a long silent moment. Logan drew in a deep breath. His gaze traveled over her shapely curves so enticingly displayed in the silky blue gown. Her skin was slightly flushed, her sapphire eyes huge as she stared back at him. Sharp little needles of longing darted through him.

"I . . . came in to check on you." His voice was husky and his tongue felt thick. He cleared his throat. "I wondered if you . . . uh, wanted something. Like toothpaste or some more towels," he added hastily.

Had he really come into her room to offer her toothpaste and towels? Krista wondered. Or did he hope to finish what he'd started last night, now that she was so handily available in his house? She'd seen the hungry way he looked at her and was instantly on her guard. "There were plenty of towels in the bathroom." Her voice shook a little. "And I brought my own toothpaste."

"I see." He continued to devour her with his eyes. "What about a drink, then? McCrory left a well-stocked bar that we're welcome to use."

"I don't want anything to drink, thank you," she said tautly.

"I'm not plotting to get you drunk in order to get

you into bed." He grimaced. "Krista, last night I made a stupid mistake in assuming that you fit my preconceived image of a—a sexually casual career woman. I'm not about to compound the damage by making a heavy pass at you while you're emotionally vulnerable."

"I'm surprised you think it's possible for a career woman to be emotionally vulnerable, Logan." She couldn't resist needling him. "Aren't we all intimidatingly strong and hard? Along with being amoral and sexually voracious, of course."

"I know what a difficult day you've had today, Krista. The anniversary grief, the shock of the burglary. I don't blame you for wanting to lash out at the most convenient target. Which happens to be me."

Her temper flared. "I know what you're doing and I don't appreciate it, Logan. Stop trying to—to handle me!"

He smiled. "I think you need a little special handling tonight, Krista. I mean that figuratively, of course."

"You'd like to mean it literally!"

"And you'd like to goad me into a quarrel? I wonder why."

"Since you're such an expert on the professional woman, I'm sure you can come up with a reason that fits all your preconceived notions."

There was another ear-splitting clap of thunder, and Krista gasped and jumped. Logan instantly crossed the room and draped a comforting arm around her. "Your nerves are shot." His fingers began to stroke the smooth, bare skin of her shoulder. "Let me get you that drink, Krista."

Her nearness was almost his undoing. Logan breathed in the fresh, feminine scent of her and swallowed hard. He wanted to curve his hand around her throat and lift her face to his. He wanted to kiss her, drinking in all her sweetness, while he pressed her soft body against his. He imagined himself cupping her breasts through the silky gown, then slipping his fingers beneath the material to tease the budding tips. Then he would pick her up in his arms and carry her to the big bed where he would caress every inch of her satiny skin. . . . But he knew he wouldn't. He couldn't, not tonight. Krista needed him in a different way tonight.

A delicious languor was spreading slowly through Krista. She wanted to lean against Logan's big body, to put her arms around him and lay her head against the reassuring warmth of his chest. To close her eyes and let the weary tension drain from her body.

As if divining her thoughts, he turned her to him and wrapped her in his arms.

"Logan, I—"

"Shh, it's all right, Krista. I'm not going to try to hustle you into bed. I just want to hold you."

Her lashes fluttered shut. That was exactly what she wanted, what she needed. "Yes, Logan, hold me," she whispered. "Hold me."

He felt her sag against him, and held her closer. An incredible wave of tenderness for her washed over him, and he felt strong and protective. She needed him. And though his body was aching, he made no sexual demands. Krista needed to be held and comforted. She needed a friend she could trust, a protector. He wanted to be whatever she needed him to be.

She slipped her arms around his waist and held on tight. She felt his warmth and strength flow into her, felt his care and concern for her. "You're right," she said. her voice was muffled by his chest. "It has been a difficult day." She sighed deeply. "I'm so tired, Logan."

"I know." His gentle hands moved slowly over her back in long, caressing strokes. His lips brushed her dark, glossy hair. "You need to sleep. Will a shot of brandy help?"

She smiled a little. "Still trying to get me drunk, Your Honor?"

"If that's what it takes to get you to sleep. I didn't come in here to seduce you, Krista."

She drew back a little and smiled up at him, her hands resting on his chest. His arms were linked loosely around her waist. She felt close to him. He had been kind to her. She'd needed him and he'd been there for her. "But you wouldn't have minded," she said lightly, "if I'd been willing to hop into bed with you, despite your good intentions."

He smiled back. "No, I wouldn't have minded at all."

She was so beautiful, she took his breath away, he thought as he stared into her glowing eyes. The urge to pull her against him and kiss her senseless was almost irresistible, but he resisted nonetheless. Krista was finally beginning to relax with him; the signs of strain were fading from her face. He didn't want to jeopardize the fragile peace between them.

"Get into bed, Krista. I'll bring a brandy up to you."

She nodded. He released her and watched her walk to the bed. His gaze followed the alluring sway of her hips as she walked, watched the smooth material glide over her body, accentuating every curve. He felt heat spread through his abdomen. He wondered if his face was flushed.

When she slipped beneath the covers he pictured himself sliding in beside her, leaning over her, learning all the sweet secrets of her body. . . . He drew a deep breath. "I'll be back with your brandy in just a few minutes."

When he returned with a snifter of cognac, he handed it to her. He would have liked to sit on the edge of her bed while she drank it, but he didn't trust himself in the undeniably tempting circumstances. The two of them, alone on a bed in a softly lit bedroom . . . He suppressed a groan at the direction his thoughts were taking. No, he didn't dare sit down on that bed.

Krista swallowed the fiery liquid and felt it burn a path from her throat to her stomach. Warmth rapidly suffused her. She glanced up at Logan. He was standing a few feet from the bed, gazing down at her with deep, dark eyes. "Logan, I want to thank you for all your help tonight. For being there when I needed you."

"I'm glad I was there for you, Krista," he said quietly. His gaze held hers for a moment, then swept over her softly flushed cheeks and the fullness of her parted lips. "I learned another lesson tonight, you know."

"Another lesson?"

His mouth curved into a wry smile. "Another lesson in the hazards of stereotyping. I'd always assumed that a bright, successful, and independent career woman didn't need anybody."

She managed to smile. "Someday you're going to come to the startling conclusion that we intimidating career women are human, after all."

"You really needed me tonight, Krista," he said almost wondrously. "I didn't think you had any needs. Drives, yes, but never needs. You're such a capable, impressive woman, Krista."

"And you much prefer twenty-two-year-olds who are dying to get married and quit their boring jobs."

Logan thought of Amy Sue Archer and frowned. Was the shapely young blonde really what he wanted? She didn't arouse his physical passion and they had nothing in common, he admitted to himself. Was he the man of Amy Sue's dreams, or did she secretly view him simply as a meal ticket? He stared into Krista's deep blue eyes, feeling terribly confused.

He didn't know it, but Krista was equally confused. Of course she wanted to be strong rather than weak. But what if her strengths and capabilities were what drove men—Logan—away? Would she have to play the simpering miss, devalue her professional abilities, change herself into something she wasn't to have a man's love? It seemed a bleak choice, one Krista knew she couldn't make.

"I'd better leave so you can get some sleep," Logan said quietly. He was exhausted himself. It seemed that nothing was the way he'd believed it to be. He felt as if the world had turned upside down since he'd first laid eyes on Krista Conway. "Good night, Krista."

"Good night, Logan."

He walked slowly to the door.

"Logan, I don't have an alarm clock with me," Krista said suddenly. "Will you or one of the kids knock on my door around seven tomorrow morning?"

He gave a quick nod and left the room. Krista settled back against the pillows. She was beginning to feel the sedating effects of the cognac. The storm continued to rage outside, but she no longer tensed at the rolls of thunder and flashes of lightning. Her mind drifted into pleasant oblivion and her eyelids closed heavily. Within a very short while, Krista fell into a deep, dreamless sleep.

When Krista awakened, the room was bright from the shaft of sunlight pouring through a gap in the curtains. She rolled onto her back and stretched luxuriously. She'd slept soundly all night and felt fit and well rested and bursting with energy.

Then she happened to glance at her watch. It was ten forty-five! She sat up with a gasp. She'd never slept so long and so late in her entire life! What had happened to the seven A.M. knock at her door that she'd requested? Had she slept through it? Or had Logan and the children forgotten to call her?

Krista leaped from the bed and rushed out into

the hall, looking for a phone. The house was empty, of course. It was a Friday, and Logan was at the courthouse and the children were at school. She found a telephone in the kitchen. Tao and Ink were there, too. Ink was sunning himself on the window-sill. Tao ran to greet her with a conversational meow.

Krista quickly dialed her office. "Vicky," she said breathlessly when her secretary, Vicky Bailey, picked up the phone. "I—"

"Oh, hi, Krista," Vicky greeted her. "Are you feel-ing better? Judge Moore called earlier to say you wouldn't be in the office this morning, and he told me all about the robbery at your place last night. That's a shame, Krista! I hope they catch the guys responsible."

"Logan called you to say I wouldn't be in this morning?" Krista echoed incredulously.

"Mmm-hmm. He said you needed to rest after what you'd been through yesterday and to cancel all your appointments for this morning. Will you be coming in at one or should I cancel your afternoon appoint-ments, too?"

"He told you to cancel my morning appointments?" Krista repeated in an incredulous squeak. *Logan Moore deliberately had decided not to wake her this morning!* Moreover, he'd taken it upon himself to call her office and instruct her secretary to cancel her appointments!

She was stunned by the sheer audacity of the man. And then she was outraged! "Don't cancel my afternoon appointments, Vicky. I'm on my way to the office now. But first I'm going to stop by the courthouse. I'll see you within the hour."

How dare Logan Moore make decisions concern-ing her! she thought as she stomped up the stairs. How dare he give her secretary orders! The incredi-ble nerve of the man! She showered and dressed in a record number of minutes, fairly throwing on the oyster-gray suit and pink silk blouse she'd brought with her last night. She couldn't remember ever being so furious in her life.

She arrived at the courthouse twenty minutes later, and her anger had not abated one whit. She strode to the suite of offices that comprised Judge Logan Moore's chambers. It suddenly dawned on her that Logan might be hearing a case in court, and she scowled fiercely. This was a confrontation that could *not* be postponed! If necessary, she would go into the courtroom and demand a recess. Then Logan could experience firsthand how it felt to have someone else interfere with your professional schedule!

"Is Judge Moore in?" she demanded of the young law clerk who was sitting at a desk piled high with briefs.

"Yes, he's back in his office," replied the clerk, "Er, do you have an appointment to see him?"

"No!" Krista said, and started back to the judge's inner chambers. The clerk stared after her and wisely decided not to interfere.

Krista flung open the door and strode into the office, banging the door shut behind her. Wearing his black judicial robes, Logan was seated at a big mahogany desk, poring over several volumes that lay open on the desktop.

He looked up and smiled as she entered. "Good morning, Krista."

"You mean 'good afternoon'!" she snarled. "Because that's what it is, you know, afternoon! And thanks to you, I missed all my morning appointments."

Logan's smile never wavered. "I looked in on you this morning at seven, and you were sleeping so soundly I decided not to awaken you. You needed the sleep more than you needed to be in your office, Krista."

She clenched her fists. His unapologetic assumption that he could decide what she needed was wildly infuriating. "You had no right to make that decision for me, Logan Moore. I told you I wanted to get up at seven and I meant it. I wanted to go to my office this morning. I wanted to see my clients!"

"I'm sure you'll have no trouble rescheduling your clients, Krista," he said in a kindly paternal tone that made her grind her teeth with vexation. "You needed to sleep. You look wonderfully well rested today. All the strain and tension and exhaustion are gone from your face. Admit it, Krista. You feel—"

"I feel like screaming! Don't you understand the point I'm trying to make?"

"Come here and tell me about it," he said invitingly. He pushed back the chair from his desk and swiveled it toward her, extending his hand to her.

She stared. He couldn't expect her to sit on his lap?

Apparently he did. When she made no move toward him, he sprang from the chair, seized her wrist, and sat back down again, pulling her down on top of him.

"Logan!" she gasped. Her rage had been abruptly supplanted by the shock of finding herself on the lap of a judge in his chambers. She tried to scramble up, only to have his arms clamp around her as securely as a steel vise.

His lips brushed the sensitive curve of her neck, sending little shivers along her spine. "Now," he said huskily, "you were saying?"

She glanced down at her slim gray skirt. It had ridden halfway up her thighs. The thick material of his black robe brushed her skin as he slid one big hand along the long, smooth length of her leg. She forgot her original complaint and focused on the newer, more urgent one. "Let me up, Logan!"

He grinned, thoroughly unrepentant. "Not until you give me a good-morning kiss."

"Have you lost your mind?" she managed to say in a choked voice.

"No, indeed." Both of his hands were now roaming freely over her, stroking from waist to thigh. "In fact, my mind is quite clear. Last night was a revelation to me, Krista."

His head lowered and he nuzzled her nose with his. "You were sleeping as soundly as a baby when I looked in on you this morning." He nipped at her lips with his, then soothed them with his tongue. "You were lying on your back with your arms resting on the pillow on either side of your head, and you looked as sweet and innocent as a baby. A beautiful, trusting baby."

Krista could feel the heat and the strength of his body enveloping her in a sensuous cocoon. She felt herself growing warm and languid under his caressing hands. "L-Logan," she protested weakly.

"You need me." His voice was deep, and his mouth brushed hers as he spoke. "And I'm going to take care of you, sweetheart." His palm moved on her thigh, learning the shape of it through the delicate nylon.

Krista had an audacious desire to feel the warmth of his hand on her bare skin. Her own hands were braced against his shoulders, ostensibly to push him away. Instead, she slowly, involuntarily began to relax.

"Logan, this is—highly irregular, to say the least," she said in a breathless voice she hardly recognized as her own. "If someone comes in . . ."

"Nobody enters a judge's chambers without knocking and gaining permission first," he said. He smiled against her lips. "Perhaps I should amend that to, nobody but Krista Conway. But that's all right, sweet. Our relationship entitles you to certain rights and privileges."

"We don't have a relationship. We haven't known each other long enough," she protested, but even to her own ears she sounded weak and unconvincing.

He was kissing her, he was caressing her, and she was growing softer and hotter and wilder. She was beginning to forget all sense of time and place. Without conscious thought, she tightened her hold on his shoulders and pressed closer to him.

"I agree that it's moved very quickly between us," he murmured, his voice soft and seductive, "but time isn't a reliable factor in determining the depth of involvement, Krista."

His words cut into her spinning mind. She stiffened, suddenly uneasy with the turn this conversation had taken. "This is beginning to sound like yet another approach to get me into bed," she said.

"Suppose I agree to allow you to decide when we'll make love? Will you lower your guard and relax with me, sweetheart?"

"You'll *agree* to *allow* me to decide?" she repeated incredulously. Incensed by his high-handed decree, she tried to escape the strong, black-robed arms holding her captive on his lap. "You're not allowing or agreeing to anything, Logan Moore. *I'm* the one who decides when and if we make love."

Her struggles didn't faze Logan in the slightest. "I believe that's what I just said," he agreed calmly.

"But with some very important differences!"

"Typical attorney, aren't you, love? Quibbling over semantics." He smiled indulgently at her. "We both have rights and privileges in this relationship, Krista. I exercised one of my rights this morning when I made the decision to let you sleep rather than awakening you to go to the office."

He brushed his mouth against hers, tickling her lips with his. "And I do have that right, Krista. Yes, everything is perfectly clear to me now."

"Oh, is it?" It was difficult to sound stern while responding to his little biting kisses.

"Mmm-hmm. You aren't the hard-boiled career woman I originally thought you were. In fact, I'm willing to bet that the stereotypical career woman doesn't exist at all. She's merely an unfortunate myth perpetrated by men who haven't yet discovered the truth."

Krista sat absolutely still. "The truth that you've discovered?" she concluded apprehensively.

"Yes. A successful, ambitious professional woman needs a man as much as any traditional woman, maybe even more so."

She drew in her breath sharply. "Needs a man?" she repeated carefully.

"Precisely. Regardless of how high her income and her professional status, a woman needs a man to lean on and take care of her. And the more assertive and independent she seems, the more she actually needs a man's guidance and protection."

"A man's guidance and protection?" Krista's voice rose a little. Her eyes were wide with incredulity. "Women, no matter how independent and successful, need to be dominated by men? Is that what you're saying, Logan?"

"Yes," he said happily. "As I said before, it's all so clear to me now, I only wonder why I didn't realize it sooner."

"Logan," she howled. "All you've done is replace one stupid chauvinistic notion with another one! An independent woman is neither a hard, sexually promiscuous villain, nor some needy creature who requires a man's domination."

"Not just any man," Logan agreed. "For instance, the only man you need is me."

Krista stared up at him. She'd come to a similar conclusion herself. And he'd used it against her two nights ago, she reminded herself. But so much had happened since then. Things were different now. Or were they?

She knew she had to find out. "That puts you in a rather awkward position, doesn't it, Logan? What happens if the only man I allegedly need is you, but the woman *you* need is sweet Amy Sue?"

"Krista, I don't feel like talking about Amy Sue at this particular time."

"Never discuss one woman while holding another one prisoner on your lap? Is that another credo in your macho code?" she asked caustically.

"What do you want me to say, Krista? That I don't need Amy Sue?" He looked thoughtful. "That I think I needed the *idea* of her—a sweet, compliant little woman with no needs or demands of her own?"

"Such a woman doesn't exist, Logan. Except in male fantasies. Men's magazines have made a fortune exploiting the myth of the girl-woman with a pea brain whose only function in life is to satisfy her big, strong macho master."

Logan had the nerve to laugh. "Hmm, it doesn't sound too bad at that."

"Which is precisely why you and I make our living in divorce court, Your Honor. A man thinks he's marrying this fantasy woman and the woman, for reasons of her own, plays the role . . . for a while. When reality surfaces, both feel cheated. Then comes the bitterness."

Logan nodded. "So you're suggesting that a man tailor his fantasies to real life? Alter his concept of the dream girl to match the opinionated, stubborn, and argumentative woman she really is?" He flashed a wicked grin.

Krista's heart did a somersault. Did she dare think Logan was trying to tell her . . . She lazily traced her finger along the strong curve of his jaw. "I can see you're not in the mood for a serious discussion on the sociological ramifications of male-female expectations and perceptions in today's culture."

He caught her hand and pressed her palm against his lips. "No, sweet. I'm in the mood for something else entirely."

Her pulses leaped, and there was a delicious tightening in her abdomen. "Logan," she whispered, and his eyes met hers. Their gazes locked, and his mouth slowly descended toward hers.

His lips had barely touched hers when a heavy knock sounded on the wood-paneled door. "Judge Moore?" called the bailiff. "Everyone is back in the courtroom."

Krista tensed and frantically tried to get off Logan's lap. "Let me up!" she whispered nervously. For an attorney to be caught on a judge's lap was a scandalous situation! She had managed to forget who and what they were, along with where they were. An alarming and unprofessional lapse on her part, she thought worriedly.

Logan reluctantly released her. "No one will come in without my permission," he said again as she stood.

She straightened her clothes with nerveless fingers. He watched her, his lips curved into a possessive smile. "Krista, about your date tonight . . ."

Good Lord, she did have a dinner date tonight! With Tom Kearny, an attorney she'd met at a trial lawyers' association meeting. She threw Logan a mutinous look. Although she might prefer to spend the evening with him, she was not going to break her date because he ordered her to do so. She had no intention of reinforcing his stupid theory of masculine dominance.

"Have your date drop you off at my place afterward," Logan said smoothly. "Your house is still a wreck and I don't want you spending the night there. The kids and I will help you fix it up this weekend, but tonight you're staying with us again."

She gaped at him. "I will not!"

"I'll see you tonight, Krista. And not too late. Be in before midnight." He dropped a quick, hard kiss on her mouth, then strode to the door.

After he'd gone, Krista thought of all the things she should have said. During the drive to her office, she demolished Logan with her scathing rebuttal of his completely intolerable, high-handed arrogance. She told him to save his caveman tactics for that living, breathing Barbie doll, Amy Sue, who just might put up with him in exchange for a lifetime supply of cash. Oh, she was Krista Conway at her courtroom best. If only Logan had been around to hear her.

Eight

"Krista, Ross Perry is on the line." Vicky Bailey's voice came through the small office intercom, and Krista laid down the packet of mail she'd been about to read and switched on the extension. "Hello, Ross," she said crisply.

"Krista, is it worthwhile for Gary Landau and me to meet with you and Marcia once more, or would it be a total waste of time?" As usual, Ross came straight to the point. He was not one to waste time with social chatter during business hours. "Even though we have our court date, I thought we ought to consider settling this thing out of court just one last time."

"We've been given a court date for the Landau trial?" Krista asked. This was news to her.

"It was confirmed by mail this morning."

"That explains it." She grimaced. "I haven't had a chance to look at my mail yet." She decided not to mention the reason why. A workaholic like Ross Perry would think she'd gone mad, sleeping till ten forty-five and missing an entire morning of appointments. "Who's the judge?"

What if it were Logan? she wondered. Her stomach knotted. It wouldn't be ethical for him to hear a case in which she was representing either party. Despite their disagreement over the extent of their personal involvement, they had to concur on one issue. Neither was capable of judging the other objectively.

"The judge is Candace Flynn," Ross said gloomily. "She'll probably decide to split little Julie in two, à la King Solomon."

Krista sighed. "It's going to take a King Solomon to rule on this case. I've never seen two people so completely obsessed with winning custody as Gary and Marcia Landau. I can't imagine what either one will do if they lose."

"The sooner it's over, the better for little Julie, though. This bouncing back and forth between her parents from day to day is not a satisfactory solution."

Krista thought of little Julie Landau, a solemn, nervous child who had been spending alternate days with each parent since their acrimonious divorce. "The only thing holding the poor child together is knowing both parents are so determined to have her. It worries me, Ross."

"Me, too. I have this altruistic fantasy of working with you to reconcile the Landaus. It's too bad Logan Moore didn't draw this case. He might've done just that." Ross chuckled.

Krista was amazed to find herself blushing. She was deeply thankful she was alone in her office, and that the astute Ross Perry was unable to observe her telling reaction to the mention of Logan's name.

"So, shall we get together with the Landaus or not?" Ross asked.

"I'd have to say no, Ross. Marcia won't yield one iota, and the last time the four of us got together—"

"It was a fiasco. Well, since my client is as set on sole custody as yours, I guess we'll see each other in court, Krista."

The Landau case was uppermost in Krista's mind

as she drove home from the office several hours later. Neither Marcia nor Gary Landau would hear of a joint custody compromise, yet there was really no reason to grant sole custody to either parent. Krista had spent hours listening to Marcia Landau rant and rave against her ex-husband, but had found no evidence that he was an unfit parent. Ross Perry had reported a similar situation with his client.

Krista sighed. For Julie Landau's sake, she almost wished Logan *were* assigned to the case. He was a parent himself, was an understanding and compassionate man. He wouldn't be swayed by the clever semantics and craftsmanship of little Julie's parents' attorneys.

Logan would rule in what he felt were the child's best interests, and he probably would have a fairly good feel for what that might be. Not so Candace Flynn. Krista had the unhappy feeling that Judge Flynn would be floundering along with her and Ross on this case.

Krista entered her house, stared at the ransacked living room, and felt queasy. She thought of Logan's order that she spend the night at his house, but now it seemed less of an order and more of an invitation. But no, she reprimanded herself. Simply because she'd been thinking admiringly of Logan's judicial skills did not mean that she admired his misguided masculine directives.

"Tao! Ink!" She called the cats, then immediately remembered they weren't there. She'd been in such a rush to get to the courthouse that morning that she'd left the two cats at Logan's house. With a small sigh, she set out for the Moores'.

Neither cat, it seemed, was in a hurry to leave his temporary home. Lauren was feeding them pieces of solid white tuna from the can as they lounged on the dining room table. Krista shooed both cats down from the table and instructed Lauren to put the food in their respective plastic dishes in the kitchen. "And make the most of the tuna fish," she warned the felines, "because it's back to Meow Mix when you get home."

"I wish Tao and Ink could live here all the time." Lauren sighed wistfully. "I wish you lived here too, Krista."

How did one respond to that? Krista quickly hugged the girl and changed the subject. "Tell me about school. Isn't your class trip to the National Air and Space Museum coming up soon?"

"We might not get to go," Lauren said glumly. "Not enough mothers signed up to chaperone."

"Oh, dear, how many mothers signed up?"

"None. And Miss Dickson said she can't handle thirty-two of us all by herself in the museum."

"Hmm, I see her point. Why didn't any mothers sign up to chaperone?"

"The ones that aren't working have babies and little kids at home. And the school says they can't bring the little kids along on a class trip."

"That is a problem." Krista frowned. Poor Lauren, and poor Miss Dickson with a classroom full of disappointed fourth-graders on her hands. An idea sprang to her mind. "Lauren, do you think I'd qualify as a chaperone for the class? I know I'm not a mother, but I do have a flexible office schedule. As long as the trip didn't fall on a day that I'm supposed to be in court, I could go along to the museum."

"I'll tell Miss Dickson on Monday!" Lauren exclaimed eagerly.

"And Lauren, let's not mention this to your father." Krista flushed a guilty pink. She was *not* encouraging the child to keep secrets from her parent, she insisted to herself. It was simply less complicated this way. "I mean, nothing is definite yet and . . ." She shrugged as her voice trailed off.

"Okay." Lauren's interest was centered on Tao, who had jumped up onto the kitchen counter to investigate the leftover pizza he found in a box there. Krista purposefully removed him from the counter and received a baleful Siamese glare.

"Krista, I can't believe you're here!" Denise said as she rushed into the kitchen, accompanied by a petite red-haired girl. "I was just going to call you. This is Heather Lincoln, a friend of mine from school. Heather, this is Krista Conway."

Krista smiled. She knew how much Denise missed her friends from Garrett County and was glad she'd found a friend at her new school. "I'm pleased to meet you, Heather."

"We have algebra and English and lunch together," Denise continued, "and we both watch *Guiding Light* after school. This is the first time Heather's been over."

"Ask her, Denise," Heather prompted in a whisper.

Krista was amused. Subtlety was obviously not Heather Lincoln's strong point. "Ask me what?"

"Heather wants me to eat dinner at her house and sleep over tonight," Denise said breathlessly. "It's okay with her mother, we already called. And it's okay with Daddy too, except he has a meeting and won't be home till later tonight. We thought Mitch would be staying with Lauren, but he just called and said he's going out for pizza and a movie with some guys from the basketball team."

"The plot thickens," Krista said dryly. "It seems there's no one to stay with Lauren, hmm?"

"Would you baby-sit her, Krista?" Denise pleaded. "Just till Daddy comes home. Please!"

"I have a dinner date tonight, Denise."

"A date?" Heather stared at Krista in astonishment. "I thought you were Denise's dad's girlfriend!"

Krista, Denise, and Lauren blushed. "Are you and Judge Moore having a fight or something?" Heather asked with interest.

There was a momentary silence. Krista recalled how she'd been regaled with tales of Awful Amy Sue from the moment she'd met the three young Moores. It was thoroughly disconcerting to think that others were being regaled with tales about her—in the role of Logan's "girlfriend"!

"I can stay by myself," Lauren announced. "I'm not scared. I'll lock the doors and watch TV. I'll be okay."

"Lauren, you can't stay alone." Denise heaved a dispirited sigh. "I can't come over, Heather. Sorry."

"Yeah, me too," Heather said.

All three girls looked thoroughly disappointed. Krista wondered why she felt she was to blame. Oh, well, what was a dinner date with Tom Kearny, after all? she asked herself. He was typical of all her dates, a pleasant, intelligent man with whom she would share dinner and light conversation and be ready to end the evening by eleven o'clock. Denise and her friend Heather looked so downcast. And Lauren looked equally glum. Krista couldn't blame her. Even at age nine, it was no fun to find yourself thrust into the role of killjoy.

"I'll call my date," she announced. "If he doesn't mind, Lauren can come along with us. If he objects, I'll break the date and stay with her."

The three girls shrieked their approval and threw their arms around Krista in an enthusiastic display of gratitude.

"She is *sooo* nice, Denise," Krista heard Heather exclaim as the two girls dashed from the kitchen. "You're *sooo* lucky to get her for a stepmother."

Lauren heard too, and she shrugged her small shoulders and smiled angelically at Krista. It was undoubtedly the same sort of smile she and her siblings flashed when they were diabolically concocting a scheme involving Amy Sue. Krista hastily excused herself to call Tom.

Tom Kearny was a genuinely nice man, Krista decided as he drove her and Lauren back to the Moores' house at twenty to eleven that evening. He had good-naturedly agreed to bring Lauren along to dinner with them at the exclusive La Fleur restaurant, not even questioning Krista's explanation that she was baby-sitting her neighbor's child due to a family emergency.

Yes, he was a *very* nice man. He didn't cringe when Lauren insisted on ordering a hamburger rather than sampling any of the spectacular French cuisine, and he merely smiled when she took one look at his dinner of lamb with black butter and mustard and said, "Yuck!" He even attempted to take part in the child-centered conversation during the meal, before he finally lapsed into silence.

Nor had he balked at Krista's suggestion that she pay for her and Lauren's dinners. It was refreshing to meet a man who didn't have any macho hang-ups about sharing the bill, Krista reminded herself. When she'd tried to pay her share at the seafood restaurant the other night, Logan had refused in no uncertain terms.

Tom Kearny also didn't follow traditional etiquette, which required a gentleman to open the car door for a lady, then escort her to her front door. Krista recalled that Logan had been careful to mention those old courtesies to Mitch, while practicing them himself. Tom called his good-byes from behind the wheel of his sporty silver-gray Maserati and was gone well before Krista and Lauren reached the front door.

If there were burglars in the house, they were on their own, Krista thought, and was immediately annoyed with herself. She was not comparing Tom Kearny with Logan Moore! Tom was a nice man, and she wondered why she had no desire ever to see him again.

They heard the music as soon as they entered the house. A classic oldie, "It's all in the Game." "Daddy's home!" Lauren shouted. Logan joined them in the small entrance hall at that moment. "We're back from our date, Daddy!"

"So I see." Logan picked Lauren up and swung her high in the air before setting the giggling girl back on her feet. "I found your note taped to the refrigerator. It was very kind of Krista to include you in her dinner plans, wasn't it? I hope you thanked her."

"Oh, yes," Lauren assured him. "And I thanked Tom, too."

"Tom?" Logan raised his brows. His eyes met Krista's, and to her consternation, she felt her face begin to grow warm. "Tom is the date, I presume? Did you like him, Lauren?" He was speaking to the child, but his ebony eyes never left Krista's.

Lauren paused, considering. "I think Amy Sue would like Tom a lot."

"You liked him that much, hmm?" Logan smiled dryly and gave her braided ponytail a tug. "It's quite late, princess. Way past your bedtime."

"Can the cats sleep in my room again tonight?" Lauren asked.

Krista opened her mouth to protest. She was going back to her house tonight and intended to take the cats with her. But before she could speak, Logan was giving Lauren his approval. "If you go up to bed right now, you can have them in your room."

"Okay!" Lauren gave her father a smacking kiss, then grabbed Krista for a quick hug. "I'll take Ink and Tao up with me right now! 'Night!"

After the departure of Lauren and the cats, Krista and Logan faced each other. Another song sounded from the stereo in the den, "Two Kinds of People in the World." "Tom, eh?" Logan said at last. "How did he like being Lauren's first date?"

"He took it in stride. And no matter what Lauren says, he does not deserve Amy Sue."

"You seem to have Amy Sue on the brain, Krista. You're always bringing her up. Today at the courthouse, tonight . . . Why the preoccupation with a twenty-two-year-old virgin who wants to quit working the moment she marries and never put in another day on any job as long as she lives?"

Krista stared at him. "She's everything you want in a woman," she couldn't resist pointing out. "You're considering marrying her."

"Yes, well . . . I'm not considering it any longer."

"You—you're not?"

"I called Amy Sue tonight, and we had along talk. Our relationship, such as it was, is now officially over." He smiled wryly. "I expect the kids will throw a party when I tell them the news."

Krista felt like joining them. She tried not to display the elation surging through her. "How did Amy Sue take the news?" she asked, hoping she sounded sufficiently solicitous.

"Very well. I think she saw the handwriting on the wall sooner than I did. She told me she knew I never would marry her when I agreed to take this position of visiting judge in Montgomery County. She said I let my children influence me too much, and she knew I'd never marry anyone they didn't like."

"I don't think you're too influenced by the kids, Logan," Krista said loyally. "You love them and don't want to hurt them, so naturally you wouldn't marry anyone they . . . uh, didn't like."

"Loathed," he corrected her. "The kids loathed Amy Sue."

"She didn't like them, either," Krista felt compelled to add.

"Well, Amy Sue's new prospect is far more suitable for her. He's a widowed doctor whose children are grown and married."

"Her new prospect?" Krista's eyes widened. "She's already lined one up?"

"Amy Sue isn't one to let grass grow under her feet. As soon as I told her I was going to Montgomery County for a year, she began to date Malcolm Chester, one of Garrett County's most successful surgeons. He's at least forty years her senior. Of course, she didn't mention it to me until tonight. Apparently, the romance has heated up since I left."

"Now she'll make sure the heat is turned up to blow-torch intensity. Has she handed in her resignation from the work force yet?"

"I imagine it's just a matter of time. Do you think she views Mal Chester as a meal ticket, Krista?" Logan asked seriously.

Krista suppressed a smile. Had she ever met a man so baffled by women? It was almost endearing— when it wasn't maddening. "I think Amy Sue has fallen head over heels for the man, Logan. She undoubtedly was swept away by his successful-surgeon's income and his lack of family fiscal responsibilities."

"Hmm, that's what I thought."

"You're so perceptive, Logan." She smiled sweetly. "How could I ever have imagined that you didn't understand women?"

He caught her hand and pulled her slowly toward him. "There's one woman I want to understand. She earns a lot of money, but she's generous and not at all materialistic. She's reached the top of her profession and lives alone, but she isn't afraid to admit she needs people. She handles divorce cases with the detail and finesse of a general mapping out war strategy, yet she's a romantic who refuses to indulge in superficial sexual encounters because she's holding out for . . . love?"

His voice lowered as he drew her nearer. "She's such a combination of paradoxes, is it any wonder I keep coming up with all the wrong conclusions? And then she gets angry or hurt, and who can blame her?"

"Oh, Logan!" Krista leaned forward and in a purely spontaneous gesture wound her arms around his neck and kissed his cheek.

She felt his body tense for a split second, then his arms came around her to hold her close. It took a supreme act of will for Logan to keep up that platonic embrace when every instinct he possessed screamed for him to kiss her until they both were reeling, to tear off the delicate pearl buttons on her butter-yellow dress and take her breasts in his hands, to bring her nipples to aching peaks of sensitivity with his mouth.

He wanted to forget that Mitch and Lauren were upstairs in their rooms, probably still very much awake. He wanted to sweep Krista into his arms and carry her to his bed, brushing aside any protests that it was too soon or too much or too risky.

He stifled a groan. Who was this sensual, passionate stranger who dwelled within the calm and balanced man he'd thought himself to be? He dropped his arms and reluctantly stepped away from Krista. There was a different song playing now—Brook Benton's rhythmic rendition of the old standard "Fools Rush In." How apropos, he thought wryly. He was living his life according to song titles.

Krista's face was flushed. The lyrics of the song drifted through her muddled mind, and she cast a covert glance at Logan. She knew he wanted her, his physical symptoms of arousal were blatantly evident. But she wanted more. She wanted him to be in love with her . . . because she loved him.

Krista was shocked at her own silent revelation. Her common sense argued against the possibility of falling in love with a man she'd known such a short time, a man who had completely misjudged her character. She tried to tell herself it was merely sexual attraction she felt for him, but every instinct told her it was much more than that. She was accustomed to trusting her instincts. Her intuitive and perceptive skills had been honed in her professional life. And now all her instincts, intuitions, and perceptions were telling her she was in love with Logan Moore.

They faced each other in silence, both floundering in a sea of confusion. "Since it's getting late, I'll be on my way." Krista said quietly. "I'll leave the cats here for tonight and pick them up tomorrow."

Logan shrugged, as if to dismiss the subject. "I want to thank you for enabling Denise to go to her friend's house and Mitch to go out with the guys. It's been hard for them, changing schools. I'm glad they're making some new friends."

. "So am I."

"Of course, I would've preferred you to cancel your date and stay here with Lauren rather than dragging the child along and keeping her out till all hours of the night, but—"

"*What?*" Krista interrupted, hardly able to believe what she was hearing.

"To your credit, you did as you were told and were in before midnight," he finished. He was grinning and his black eyes were alight with laughter.

"You're teasing me, you cretin!"

"I knew you were quick on the uptake, counselor." He caught her hand. "I have a bottle of chardonnay chilling in the refrigerator. Let's have a glass and go to bed. Separate beds of course," he added, "in our separate rooms."

"Logan, I really can't stay tonight."

He was pulling her along to the kitchen. "I'm not letting you spend the night alone in a house with locks that already have been proven to be inadequate. Tomorrow we'll call a locksmith and have all new locks installed, and the windows secured as well. The kids and I will help you get the place back in order. But tonight you're staying here. End of discussion."

They were in the kitchen now and he lifted her onto one of the high stools that lined the breakfast bar. "You're terribly pushy, Judge Moore," she informed him.

"I believe the word you want is 'masterful,' counselor."

"Will you settle for overbearing or domineering instead?" But she was smiling as she spoke.

"Objection overruled." Once again he was struck by the forceful combination of her warmth and beauty. The rich yellow color of her dress enhanced her milk-white complexion and set off the striking contrast of her dark, dark hair.

Shaking his head, he turned away from her so he wouldn't grab her.

He poured two glasses of the chilled wine and set one in front of her. "About this Tom person—your date tonight?"

"Yes?" Krista took a sip of the wine.

"I don't want you seeing him again."

She raised her brows. "Just like that? You tell me you don't want me to see Tom again and you expect me to obey you?"

Logan drained the contents of his glass. "Yes."

"All right."

He stared at her. "I don't want you to see *any* other men, Krista," he added, watching her with an air of tense expectancy.

"I won't," she said softly, simply.

Logan poured himself another glass of wine. "I guess only saccharinely sweet twenty-two-year-olds bent on marriage and a meal ticket like to have several men on the string at the same time."

"It does tend to widen a girl's options," Krista agreed dryly. "Quite an important factor in the meal-ticket market."

Logan shook his head again. "I've been an idiot, Krista."

She flashed a grin. "At least you're man enough to admit it."

"And you're a generous woman to forgive me for it. You have forgiven me, haven't you?"

"Absolutely."

They smiled at each other. Conversation turned to the courtroom. Krista told Logan about the upcoming Landau case, and they discussed various other custody cases they'd been involved in. They traded law school stories and talked about their mutual interest in family law. Krista marveled over Logan's appointment to the bench at the young age of thirty, Logan was equally impressed by the successful practice Krista had built at relatively the same age.

"But why specialize in divorce?" he asked. "What made you decide to become a . . . barracuda?" It was a question that had plagued him since he'd first laid eyes on her. She hadn't looked the part, and now he knew she didn't act the part in her personal life, either.

"I found the divorce laws biased and even prejudicial," she said, "and I thought a good matrimonial lawyer could make a stunning difference. I wanted a chance to prove it. When I went directly from law school into practice with my brother and his partner, I asked to handle the divorce cases. Since those were their least favorite cases, Eric and Craig were delighted to oblige." Krista smiled in reminiscence. "After the cut-and-dried textbook cases in law school, I found handling divorces for clients a revelation. In every case I played a variety of roles—psychiatrist, confessor, accountant, referee, and detective. And I discovered that I had a knack for it."

"That's certainly true."

"I wanted to right some of the wrongs I saw in the divorce laws. There are some clients I refuse to take." Her eyes met Logan's. "Wilson Marshall and his kind, for example. I don't like to straddle the fence on moral issues either, you see."

Logan held her gaze. "I had no call to make that accusation, Krista. I apologize for it. Please continue."

She gave an acknowledging nod. "Candace Flynn was renowned as the premier divorce lawyer in this area. When she was appointed to the bench five years ago, I seem to have inherited her title as chief barracuda." Krista shrugged. "I was glad to lose myself in work. After Eric's and Craig's deaths, there didn't seem to be anything else."

"I know. If I hadn't had the kids to come home to after Beverly's death, I probably would've lived in my office at the courthouse."

"How did she die, Logan?" Krista asked softly.

"Kidney disease. She developed glomerulonephritis from a strep infection and it ravaged her kidneys. Bev was one of the few who couldn't tolerate dialysis." He stared blindly, remembering. "She was slipped to the head of the list for a kidney transplant, but it was too late. She was desperately ill and too weak to survive the operation."

Krista reached across the counter and grasped his hand in silent empathy. For a moment, neither spoke. Both were lost in their memories.

Krista was the first to break the silence. "You've done a wonderful job with the children," she said. "They're great kids."

"I think so, too." He smiled. "And I suppose Amy Sue was right. There's no way I would marry if it made my kids unhappy. Their happiness comes first with me."

"It's refreshing to hear a parent say that. So often I hear my clients say that their own happiness comes first and their children will just have to adjust."

"The Bolgers. That's why I decided to put their children first. Someone had to."

Krista arched her brows. "Let's agree to disagree on your *Bolger* v. *Bolger* ruling, Your Honor."

The cuckoo clock in the kitchen struck twelve, and the tiny wooden bird burst out of a small door to cuckoo twelve times. Krista and Logan watched, grimacing. They laughed at their mutual reaction to the noisy little bird.

"Let's feed him to the cats," Logan suggested.

"Good idea. But I don't think Bill McCrory would like it."

They agreed then to let the bird live, but Logan

resolved not to wind the clock for the remainder of his year's stay.

They walked upstairs together and paused to look in on Lauren, who was sound asleep with both cats stretched across the foot of her bed. Mitch's door was closed, but light shone from the crack under the door and the muffled sound of rock music drifted into the hall.

"Not your kind of music," Krista said to Logan, smiling.

"I listen to music. Mitch and Denise listen to noise."

"ZZ top is not noise!" Mitch called from behind the door.

Krista laughed. Logan groaned. "I remember when the kids were very small," he said, "Bev and I would tuck them in bed at seven-thirty and have the entire evening to ourselves. Now there are nights when Mitch stays up later than I do." A teenage son, awake and liable to emerge from his room at any given moment, was an extremely effective chaperone, Logan added to himself.

He walked Krista to the door of the bedroom she'd used the night before. "I left my nightgown and toothbrush and the rest of my things here," she said, thinking of her manic rush to leave for the courthouse that morning. "I thought I'd take it all back with me tonight."

A knot of tension was pulsing in her abdomen. They were standing outside her bedroom door and the situation reminded her of two teenagers on a date, prolonging the end of the evening by talking on the porch step while trying to gather up the courage to kiss good night.

Merely the mention of Krista's nightgown sent Logan's brain spinning with images of the way the ice-blue silk had sensuously molded itself to her soft curves. A flash of heat surged through him. He couldn't stand here making idle small talk for another second. He had to touch her, had to . . .

He took her hand and pulled her gently into the room. He closed the door and turned to face her, holding both her hands in his. "One good-night kiss?" He'd intended to sound light and casual. He was fully aware that he sounded anything but.

Krista heard the throb in his voice, saw the desire flare in his ebony eyes. She managed a tremulous smile. "Perhaps just one."

His mouth closed over hers, claiming it for his own in a hungrily passionate, possessive kiss. Krista shifted and sighed, her body softening in his arms as she invited him deeper and deeper into the sweet warmth of her mouth. This was what she had been wanting, *needing* . . . Logan, only Logan.

She made a small sound in the back of her throat as his tongue slid over hers, rubbing and stroking, luring it into the moist depths of his mouth. As she clung to him, her arms wrapped around his neck, he drew back slightly and cupped her breasts. They surged and swelled, filling his hands.

His mouth held hers and his thumbs moved lightly over her nipples, which were taut and sensitive and straining against the soft cloth of her dress. He caressed the protruding buds until they were hot and engorged.

Krista moaned. She felt herself tumbling out of control with an astonishing swiftness. It was incredibly exciting, being touched only on her mouth and her nipples. Sensual anticipation built. She wished her breasts were bare. She imagined Logan soothing her tight, hard nipples with his mouth and tongue, and a liquid heat flooded her at the wanton thought.

She wanted more and more. She arched into him, rubbing her hips against him, inflaming and frustrating them both with the clothing that lay between them. Finally, Logan took her hips in his hands and ground her against his burgeoning masculinity.

"I want you," he said fiercely. "I feel like I'm burning up with it. I want to pick you up and carry you straight to bed." He sighed heavily. "But I can't." His hands skimmed the tight curve of her buttocks. "And it's pure torture."

"I know," she whispered. "It's neither the time nor the place."

"Oh, it's the time, all right." His laugh was hoarse. "It's the place that's all wrong. The kids . . ."

"Anyway, we agreed on one good-night kiss. Sort of a verbal contract, as it were." She stood on her toes and kissed his cheek, then stepped away from him. It was no use prolonging the inevitable. She and Logan might be spending the night under the same roof, but they weren't spending it in the same bed. "And we've fulfilled the terms of that contract, haven't we, Your Honor?"

"I'd like to rule against you on this one, counselor."

She blew him a kiss as she stepped into the adjoining bathroom. "Good night, Logan."

"Good night, sweetheart," he said softly as he left the room. As he started down the hall he heard footsteps on the stairs and frowned. "Mitch?"

Mitch trudged up the steps, carrying a plate with a towering sandwich stacked on it in one hand and a huge glass of milk in the other. He joined his father on the landing. "Hi, Dad. What are you doing here?"

"I'm about to go to bed. And you're about to have nightmares if you eat that concoction at this hour."

Mitch shrugged. "I'm starving." He sidled closer to Logan and lowered his voice to a conspiratorial whisper. "Are you going to Krista's room, Dad?"

"I most certainly am not!"

"Hey, Dad, you're not talking to Denise or Lauren, you know. I know how it is between men and women."

Logan arched his brows. "Oh, you do, do you?"

"Sure. Krista is gorgeous, Dad. And she's nice and

she's rich. She can get any guy she wants. So you'd better, you know, grab her while you can."

Logan drew himself to his full six feet four inches and purposefully looked down on his son. "Mitch, I assume you mean well, but I neither need nor will accept advice on women from my sixteen-year-old son."

"I think Krista really likes you, Dad," Mitch insisted. "You gotta make your move!"

"Good night, Mitchell," Logan said pointedly.

Mitch looked as if he were about to say more, but the expression on his father's face stopped him. "Good night, Dad." Juggling the sandwich and the milk, he went into his bedroom and closed the door.

Logan stood in the hallway, staring from Krista's closed bedroom door, to Mitch's, to his own, his son's words echoing through his head. *"Krista can get any guy she wants. So you'd better grab her while you can."*

What would a beautiful, successful—and yes, rich—woman like Krista want with a man who had three kids and a far lesser income than she earned herself? She was a woman who could have any man she wanted.

Logan stared from door to door for a long time. Sex, he decided. The sexual chemistry between them was exciting and explosive, as unique and addictive to Krista as it was to him. She wasn't a woman who indulged in affairs, but she wanted one with him.

He wondered why he wasn't elated by the knowledge. Then he admitted the truth to himself. He wanted something far more than an affair with her. Something lasting, something permanent. He wanted to live with her, he wanted to share his family with her. He wanted her to bear him a child. His lips curved into a small smile. He loved kids and was a sucker for little babies. To have a child or two with Krista . . .

His smile faded abruptly. It was an impossible

dream, of course. There could be no permanence in his relationship with Krista Conway. He was to be in Montgomery County for one year only. His life and his ties were in Garrett County, and Krista was well established here. She had a two-hundred-fifty-thousand-dollar-a year career based here. A woman didn't give up that kind of career and income. *No one* gave up that kind of career or income! For anyone.

So he would settle for an affair. He would take whatever she wanted to give him and demand no more. And because he knew when it would end, he could protect himself against the pain of their inevitable parting. With a final, longing glance at Krista's bedroom door, he marched resolutely into his own room to face another night alone.

Nine

Krista and Logan spent the weekend restoring her house to its pre-burglary order. Mitch, Denise, and Lauren helped too, although Lauren spent most of the time chasing after Ink and Tao, indoors and out.

Krista ordered pizzas to be delivered for dinner on Saturday night and paid for them, despite Logan's insistence that he pay. After dinner, all of them, including the cats, returned to the Moores' house. New burglarproof locks had been ordered, but the locksmith wasn't available to install them until Monday. Logan insisted that Krista spend both nights with them, and Krista did not demur. It seemed natural to go with Logan and his children, even if it meant leaving her own home unoccupied.

When the Moores went to church on Sunday morning, Krista went along with them. After the service they drove to a nearby restaurant for a buffet brunch, Krista would've picked up that check too, except Logan literally snatched it from her hand.

By Sunday afternoon, every room in Krista's house was back in order, and she took Lauren to the local supermarket to shop for dinner. It was more rewarding to cook for a group than just for oneself,

Krista decided, as she set the roast leg of lamb, sweet potatoes, broccoli, and salad on the table. Denise helped her make a chocolate pie for dessert.

"Krista, this is great!" Mitch said enthusiastically as he helped himself to thirds of everything. "She sure is a good cook, isn't she Dad?"

"An excellent dinner," Logan agreed, trying to ignore Mitch's highly conspicuous, conspiratorial wink.

Still, he couldn't dispute his son's assertion. Krista was a good cook and it was an excellent dinner. And an expensive one. He shopped in supermarkets, he knew the going price of a leg of lamb the size and quality of this one. He thought of the strain his monthly food bills put on his budget and knew that they wouldn't make even a dent in Krista's.

Right then Tao jumped up onto the table and seized a piece of meat from Mitch's plate. Everyone laughed, and Logan joined in, putting the thought of disparate incomes aside.

The locksmith arrived on Monday afternoon to install the new locks. Krista left the office early to let him in. When Mitch, Denise, and Lauren got home from school, they saw her car parked in the driveway and came right over. She took the three of them with her to an audio/video appliance shop where she bought a new television, stereo, and VCR. Mitch was quite knowledgeable about stereos and was thrilled when she chose the elaborate model he recommended.

When Logan arrived home, he found Mitch, Denise, and Lauren each wearing headphones plugged into their individual Sony Walkmans, clipped to their belts. Krista was broiling steaks in the kitchen.

"Look, Daddy," Lauren exclaimed, holding up her small radio. "Krissy bought these for us for helping her pick out stuff at the store!"

"Stuff?" Mitch repeated. "Lauren, you don't call the kind of equipment we bought today *stuff*. Dad, Krista bought the Revox stereo system I told her about. You know, the one I read about in *Sound* magazine. I can't wait to play my new albums on it." His dark eyes were glowing with pleasure.

"I can't wait to watch *Guiding Light* on the new TV," Denise added. "Can I invite Heather over after school tomorrow to watch, Krista? Of course, I'll need a key, 'cause you aren't home then."

"Of course," Krista said as she placed the foil-wrapped baked potatoes on a platter. She reached for a large red tomato and began to slice it for the salad.

"Krista bought a twenty-seven-inch color TV," Mitch said. "It does just about everything except turn itself on."

"It turns itself off," Denise reminded him. "Remember that special sleep button? I'm the one who picked out the TV, Daddy. I just adored the great big screen!"

Logan stared from Krista to the children. He felt as if he'd come into a theater during the second act of a play and was expected to follow the story line, even though he'd missed the entire first act.

Krista turned to smile at him. "The kids went shopping with me to replace the stolen television, stereo, and VCR. And we stopped to buy some things for dinner."

"Steak, Dad. Your favorite," said Denise. "And a cherry cake for dessert."

"You bought all that electronic equipment today, Krista?" Logan asked. "But you haven't even filed your insurance claim yet." He was flabbergasted. He'd spent three months researching consumer magazines, then another several weeks pricing TV's all over Garrett County, before he'd replaced their eight-year-old television set.

Mitch answered for Krista. "She wrote a check for everything, Dad."

Logan knew the boy was dazzled. He'd been brought up in a thrifty, practical home where a major purchase was a major event. The Moores didn't buy a television and a stereo in the same *year*, let alone the same day! Once again the disparity of his and Krista's incomes was driven home to him

"Dinner's ready. Let's eat," Krista announced. The kids beat a path to the table. Logan took his place at the head of the table, and Krista handed him the big plate of steak. Their fingers touched and their eyes met. She smiled at him, and he felt as if the top of his head had been blown off.

"Any interesting cases today?" she asked. He gazed into her beautiful sapphire eyes and felt the rest of the world fade away. There were just the two of them, and she was smiling at him and serving him a delicious meal, eager to listen to the events of his day.

Logan launched into a detailed account of a difficult juvenile case he'd ruled on that morning, and because Krista was a lawyer she was able to grasp the technicalities of the case and add her own insights. He was thoroughly enjoying the stimulating discussion, when Lauren suddenly cut in.

"Krissy, I forgot to tell you. Miss Dickson picked me to pass out papers for the whole month of October!"

Logan glanced at his youngest child with uncharacteristic impatience—and was startled to discover that Lauren was looking at him in exactly the same way! Why, they were competing for Krista's attention, he realized with a slight shock. He well remembered how Lauren had refused even to speak to Amy Sue. He'd once offered the child a dollar to say hello to Amy Sue—which Lauren had turned down disdainfully.

That's wonderful, Lauren," Krista said warmly.

"And I have a note from Miss Dickson for you, too." Lauren hopped up and rushed from the room, returning a moment later with a rather crumpled sealed envelope.

Logan stared at Krista. "You have a note from Lauren's teacher?"

"Krissy is going to the museum with my class next week," Lauren said happily.

Krista glanced over the note. Her eyes widened and she read it again. Miss Dickson had addressed the note to "Mrs. Moore." And she profusely thanked her for volunteering to be the fourth-grade room mother. In addition to chaperoning the class on trips, she would be in charge of the three class parties at Halloween, Christmas, and Valentine's Day. Miss Dickson would be happy to meet with her to discuss the games and refreshments needed for the upcoming Halloween party.

Krista looked at Lauren's happy face, then back at Miss Dickson's enthusiastic note. "May I?" Logan said. He fairly snatched the note from her hands and read it. "Fourth-grade room mother?" he said incredulously.

"My office hours are flexible." Krista shrugged. "And it can't be that hard to come up with some games and refreshments for a bunch of kids, can it?"

Now Mitch had the note. "Mrs. Moore, huh?" He grinned. Denise giggled. Krista and Logan carefully avoided each other's eyes.

"This is my first time to be the room mother's child," Lauren said proudly. "The room mother's child gets to decide what kind of cookies and candy we're going to have. And to pass out the cups and napkins at all the parties."

"Mom was always room mother for Mitch and me, till she got sick," Denise said. "I always insisted she make chocolate cupcakes with pink icing for every class party every year."

"That's what I want for my class party," Lauren said quickly. "Okay, Krissy?"

Krista smiled at her. "Okay, Lauren."

"Krista has a full work schedule," Logan said. "She

doesn't have time for class trips and chocolate cupcakes and—"

"Oh, Daddy, she always has time for me," Lauren said confidently, dismissing his protests.

"Sure she does," agreed Mitch. "Right, Mrs. Moore?" All three young Moores beamed.

After dinner Logan drove Krista home in the Bentley and, ever polite, opened the car door for her and walked her to the front door. "Thank you for the dinner," he said rather stiffly. "For buying it and preparing it. As I said earlier, it was an excellent meal."

She shrugged. "I enjoyed it, too." It felt strange leaving the warmth and activity of the Moores' house to come here, to this empty place that no longer felt like home. She would have liked to have spent the evening there, but Logan had been tense since Lauren had brought out the note addressed to Mrs. Moore. He hadn't smiled when Mitch had teased about it. Obviously, the thought of being married to a career woman was too grim even to joke about.

They stepped inside. The hall light was on and the living room was in perfect order. The new television, stereo, and VCR were all in place.

Logan cleared his throat. "Krista, about this room-mother business . . ."

"I won't do it if you'd rather I didn't," she said swiftly.

"It's not that! It's just . . . Do you want to do it?"

She smiled. "I think it might be kind of fun. Of course, I'll straighten Miss Dickson out on the *Mrs. Moore.*"

Logan tried to smile. Krista thought it was funny, he realized. Cute, perhaps. The truth was, he didn't blame Lauren, and the older kids, for wanting him and Krista to get together. She was wonderful. She was fun to be with, she was thoughtful and generous and genuinely liked kids. And from a purely male point of view, she was also intelligent and passionate and sexy . . .

But would the kids be able to understand and accept that any relationship with Krista would be a limited one? *He* could handle an affair with a built-in termination date, but could his children? He didn't want them to be hurt.

"I suppose I'll have to talk to the kids," he said grimly, speaking his thoughts aloud. "They tend to think in terms of permanence, and whatever happens between you and me isn't going to be permanent. They have to understand that from the outset."

Krista swallowed. "Yes, I can see that." She'd known that Logan could be painfully blunt, but he'd outdone himself this time. *Whatever happens between you and me isn't going to be permanent.* This time he was bludgeoning her with his words. She turned away, not wanting him to see the hurt she knew she couldn't hide.

"It's important to be honest with children," Logan went on. He stared at the nape of her neck, so soft and slender and vulnerable. Heat shot through him. He wanted to kiss her there, to wrap his arms around her waist and pull her against him while he tasted her sweet warmth.

"Yes, yes, it is," she said. She was truly a romantic fool, of world-class champion caliber, she chided herself. She couldn't seem to stop weaving fantasies about herself and Logan. She'd even incorporated his children into them, just one big happy family!

"Honesty is very important," she added quietly. She couldn't accuse Logan of being dishonest with her. He'd made it plain from the day they'd met that he wanted to take her to bed. And she wanted that, too. It was just that sex was all he wanted from her while she wanted so much more from him.

The telephone rang, and for a change, Krista was as eager as Lauren to answer it—to escape from Logan and all his honesty. "If you'll excuse me, Logan." She gave him a brief, dismissing smile before racing to the phone.

Logan stood in the hall for a few moments. Krista's voice sounded crisp, efficient, and professional. Obviously, a business call, he deduced. There was no reason for him to hang around. He'd felt her withdrawing from him before the telephone had rung, while he was subtly trying to determine whether or not she wanted a short-term affair—or something more lasting—with him. Rather than denying it, she'd turned away from him when he'd suggested that a relationship between them couldn't be permanent. She probably was afraid he was about to pressure her into a commitment she didn't want to make.

Logan let himself out, taking care to pull the door firmly shut behind him. He didn't want to leave her here. For the past four nights he'd had her under his roof and he wanted her there again tonight. He wanted to know she was safe, to know that he need only cross the hall to look in on her, warm and soft and sweet, asleep in his home. Under his protection.

He longed to break down her door and drag her out of there, to bring her home with him where she belonged. For a moment, he considered doing just that. But, of course, he didn't. He was a rational, practical man, not a primitive who knocked down doors and carried off women.

Krista was an independent adult, perfectly capable of spending the night alone in her own home. With a final glance at her house, Logan began to walk slowly home.

She was restless, she couldn't sleep. Krista glanced at the clock as she climbed out of bed for the fourth time that hour. Time was creeping by, one long moment after another. It was just a little past midnight, and she felt as if morning were centuries away.

Her mind was racing. It happened sometimes. Details of her cases, of crucial countermoves and courtroom strategy had kept her awake before. Tonight, though, she wasn't thinking about her clients. She was thinking about Logan.

It had been a long time since she'd felt this way, charged-up and nervous. Tense with a peculiar anticipation and excitement. Her senses seemed more acute, her emotions reckless and volatile. She felt oddly torn between laughter and tears.

She sighed. It was going to be a *very* long night. She walked downstairs and Tao followed her, meowing, ever in hopes of a snack. Ink was already in the kitchen, crouched on the windowsill, staring inscrutably at the midnight autumn moon.

Krista refilled the cat dishes, then poured some milk in a pan to warm for herself. Wasn't warm milk the universal panacea for sleeplessness? She'd never tried it before, but perhaps it would help her tonight. It looked pretty bad, though, she thought, staring at the liquid heating in the saucepan. A thin skin was beginning to congeal on the top. And she was supposed to drink this stuff? Insomnia began to hold a little more appeal.

And then the doorbell rang. For a moment, Krista stood stock-still, wondering if she had imagined it. Who on earth would be ringing her doorbell at this hour of the night? The bell rang again, and she turned off the stove and walked to the door, more curious than alarmed. Did Federal Express deliver at this time? She *was* expecting a packet of information from a colleague on the West Coast . . .

She opened the door. Logan Moore stood before her. "Logan!" She stared, stunned by the sight of him. He was wearing a faded plaid shirt and an equally worn pair of jeans. His hair was rumpled, his face unshaven. He looked as if he'd just climbed out of bed, thrown on whatever clothes he'd found first, and . . . come to her. "What—what are you doing here?"

Logan gazed down at her. She was wearing a cranberry-colored nightgown that reminded him of a Chinese tunic, with long sleeves and a mandarin collar and buttons that ran from the neck to its mid-thigh hem.

"You didn't ask who was at the door before you opened it," he heard himself boom in the stentorian tones he used to announce a courtroom ruling. "You didn't even put on the chain when you unlocked the door. You just flung it wide open to whoever happened to be here."

"True." She moistened her lips with her tongue. "Perhaps I could lock the door again and we could take it from the top," she suggested carefully.

Instead, Logan pushed his way inside and kicked the door shut. His big hands fastened around her upper arms and he stared into her wide blue eyes. "I'm tired of always saying the wrong things to you," he said hoarsely, his eyes burning like onyx fire. "I couldn't sleep tonight, I couldn't do anything but think about you and how much I need you."

He pulled her close, closer. "I want you. I want you, want you . . ." His mouth came down fiercely on hers.

Krista's lips parted on impact, and she made a small, soft sound as his tongue surged into her mouth. The restless evening hours thinking about Logan had primed her body for his touch, and almost at once she was limp and liquid with desire.

Logan kissed her as if he were starving for her. His lips nibbled her neck. He trailed hot kisses along the line of her jaw and across her cheeks. He nipped and licked at her lips, depriving her of the hard pressure she craved until she grasped his head with her hands and captured his marauding mouth with her own.

"Krista." He breathed her name, then his mouth opened over hers and he was kissing her as she longed to be kissed, hot and hard and deep, demanding her body's most primitive, ardent responses.

She trembled, moving her hands restlessly over

him, sliding them beneath the soft material of his shirt to feel the warmth of his bare skin. The touch of her slender fingers excited him further. His blood was hot and thundered through his head.

Without a word he swept her up into his arms and carried her upstairs, his face dark with passion, his eyes glittering as he stared into her face. Her arms were linked around his neck and she rested her head against his shoulder. She nuzzled closer. He smelled of soap and faint traces of a spicy men's cologne combined with his own enticing scent. She inhaled the heady male essence and her arousal deepened.

Logan knew where her bedroom was and carried her directly to it. "I can't believe we're finally alone together," he whispered as he laid her down on the cool cotton sheets. "No kids, no cats." His lips curved into a wry grin. "I half expected that crazy Siamese to attack on the steps again."

"Tao is too interested in his midnight snack to bother with us." Krista smiled up at him. "Logan." She cupped his cheek with her hand, her fingertips gently stroking. The texture of his unshaven skin was pure male and arousing. "I was aching for you tonight. I'm so glad you're here."

There was much more she wanted to tell him, but her head was spinning and she was unable to express her thoughts coherently. She was in love with him, and for now nothing was more important than that.

"Oh, Krista." He groaned and slowly, steadily eased her onto her back. "I'm glad I'm here, too." He watched her intently as he unfastened the buttons of her gown and pushed it aside to bare her breasts.

"Your breasts are beautiful," he said huskily. "So high and firm and white." He cupped them and they overflowed in his palms. "So pretty and pink." His thumbs flicked over her nipples, which were already tight and throbbing.

Krista uttered a breathless moan and arched helplessly under his hands. He lowered his head to take one aching nipple in his mouth, and she felt a lightning-quick response deep within the feminine core of her.

She moved her hands across his back and shoulders, caressing him through the soft material of his shirt. He was so big, so hard and muscular. She loved the feel of him, but she wanted more. She wanted to touch his naked skin, to learn the different textures of his body. Her fingers fumbled with the buttons of his shirt, but she finally managed to work them loose.

Her hands tangled in the wiry-soft dark hair on his chest, then sought his hard nipples. She circled them with her fingertips, and when Logan made a wordless sound of pleasure she smiled, feeling feminine and sexy and wildly, crazily in love. She trailed her fingers from his sternum to his abdomen and found the zipper of his jeans.

Logan felt her fingers brush him and sucked in his breath sharply. He felt his control begin to skid away, and ruthlessly summoned it back. Catching her wrists, he chained her hands above her head with one of his. "We're going to take it slowly, Krista. I want to do this right. I want to make it last for a long, long time."

She struggled a little, but could not escape from his hold. Some primitive instinct wanted to challenge his insistent masculine assertion, wanted to make him lose the iron control that allowed him to hold back from her. She teased his lips with hers, brushing her mouth softly, tantalizingly over his, but withdrawing when he tried to deepen the kiss. "And that means you'll set the pace?"

"Yes, my hot little lover." He gave up trying to capture her mouth and trailed a path of stinging kisses from her throat of her breasts. He caught hold of one tight pink nipple with his mouth and circled the tip with his tongue. "I'll set the pace."

She really ought to protest that self-assured sexual declaration, Krista thought dizzily. But he was making her tremble with the wild sensations his lips and hands were arousing, and it was too difficult to worry about the balance of power in this complex relationship when she was nearly out of her head with passion.

Logan released her hands. She wrapped her arms around his neck and they kissed—long, slow voluptuous kisses that made them both shudder with need. Krista twisted in his arms, squirming with need. He teased and caressed her breasts until she cried out his name in a voice hoarse with need. She felt as if liquid fire was pouring through her body.

"Yes, yes," he murmured huskily, continuing his thrilling sensual play. "Let me hear what I'm making you feel. No one will hear those wild, sweet little noises but me."

His hand slid slowly over her stomach and his thumb explored the indentation of her navel before his fingers moved lower. Krista held her breath. She wanted him to touch her, wanted it with a shocking urgency.

His hand paused at the lace-trimmed edge of her tiny bikini panties. She closed her eyes and quivered with frustration. Yes, she silently urged him. Oh, Logan, yes!

And then his big, warm hand slipped inside her panties and his fingers stroked the downy thatch of hair before moving further, deeper . . . Krista blushed at the wetness he found there.

"So hot and sweet and wild," he whispered, pleased by the undeniable evidence of her arousal. "My passionate little Krista, you want me as much as I want you." He discovered her most sensitive and secret places, and she gasped at the intense, exquisite pleasure he evoked.

"Logan, please," she cried, and she didn't know if she were pleading with him to stop this incredibly exciting torment or begging him not to.

"Yes, darling, I want to please you," he murmured, his breath hot against her ear. He slipped his tongue inside the delicate shell at the same moment that his long fingers entered the moist heart of her femininity. The dual erotic invasion was shattering. "Tell me how. Tell me what you like."

She moaned at the intense pleasure radiating from his gentle caresses. "Just like that," she whispered, clinging to him. "Oh, Logan, it feels good. I—I—" She couldn't breathe, couldn't speak. A storm of sensual forces was gathering deep within her, and she was aching and throbbing from the intensity of it all.

Her breath came in shallow, rapid pants. She shivered and whimpered as the forces continued to build and expand, making her oblivious to everything but the tempestuous turmoil going on between her legs. Suddenly a hot burst of lightning unleashed the storm within her, and she felt herself explode into a shattering pleasure, so intense she could do nothing but cling to Logan as waves of spectacular sensation pulsed through her.

Logan held her tight, cradling her possessively against him. He whispered to her, soft sexy love words, while her body quaked and quivered in his arms. The rapture seemed to go on and on, like an electrical spark lighting a series of fuses, causing a continuous chain reaction. Krista had never experienced anything like it. Logan had shown her that she was capable of attaining heights she'd never dreamed were within the power of her own sexuality.

Finally, she lay limp and slack against him. He stared down at her flushed, damp face, and a thrill shuddered through him. He felt powerful and sexy, a man who had brought his woman supreme, sublime satisfaction. He felt tender and protective toward her, too. She had surrendered so sweetly to him, ceding all control, giving herself to him completely.

Her eyes fluttered open and she met his piercing gaze. "Logan," she murmured dazedly.

He dropped a quick kiss on her temple then gazed down at her with glittering eyes. Her unconditional surrender had heightened the urgency that had been driving him for days, intensifying his desire for her into burning all-consuming need that went far beyond the basic sexual longings of a man for a woman. It was Krista he wanted, Krista he needed. Only Krista. Her warmth, her laughter, her sweet passion. He wanted all of it, all of her.

Krista blushed scarlet. He had been watching her! She thought never had she dreamed herself capable of such a wildly uninhibited response. And they weren't even undressed yet!

"I-I don't know what happened to me," she murmured, and tried to pull away from him. Her abandon made her feel exposed and vulnerable. Logan hadn't relinquished his self-control as she had. His command of himself served to highlight her own uncontrolled response. Logan was capable of holding back. He was still holding back while she . . .

"Don't be shy with me, Krista." His hand slowly glided along the length of her body in a long, sensual caress. "You were wonderful. So responsive and passionate. So pliant and sweet." He kissed her again. "Do you know how it makes a man feel to know that he has satisfied his woman?"

She gazed into his eyes. "Happy?" she guessed, her voice soft. Could she make him lose himself in her? Could she break through the emotional barrier that still existed between them, despite their physical intimacy?

"Proud and masculine," he added, then smiled. "And very happy." He began to undress, swiftly shrugging out of his clothes and dropping them into a pile on the floor. He reached for her. "And you can make me even happier, if you want." With one deft movement he removed her nightgown, then took off her panties.

Krista stared at him with love-filled eyes, drinking in the sight of his powerful nude body. He was hard and strong, and it was obvious how much he wanted her. She held her arms open to him. "I want to, Logan. I want to make you happy."

She wanted to give him everything, to show him how very much she cared. She needed to be as close to him as she could get. She was the right woman for him in every way, Krista knew it. If only *he* would realize it!

"Come here," he commanded softly, and she went into his arms and wrapped herself around him. They kissed and kissed and incredibly, despite her earlier satiation, passion began to throb and build within her again.

Logan's body was pounding with desire. He felt as explosive as a powder keg. And Krista's hot, honeyed response was the spark that ignited him. Her thighs parted for him and he moved over her and into her with a driving thrust that filled her and inexorably forged them together.

Krista didn't think it possible that he could rouse her desire to the same fever pitch he had such a short while ago. But she was wrong, for his slow, deep movements rekindled the glowing embers of her passion. His need, his desire for her sent her soaring higher and higher, filling her, completing her. Once again she was racked by cataclysmic spasms of pleasure as Logan made love to her with an almost violent but always controlled passion.

He set the pace and the rhythm, wringing cries of ecstasy from her, possessing her body and heart and soul. A sensual explosion rocked her, deeper and stronger than before, and she clung to him and gasped his name.

Together they scaled the scorching heights of passion and hurtled onto the rapturous summit. Together they floated into a private world where tension and separation did not exist, only the peaceful bliss of completion.

Afterward, they lay in each other's arms, sated and silent in the warm afterglow of passion. Logan replayed their lovemaking in his mind. It had been wonderful, all he had expected and more. For a few shattering moments, he'd almost totally lost himself to her, and that was a risk he didn't dare take, not in this temporary affair.

He mustn't trick himself into believing it could last forever; he must take precautions to steel himself for the end. At his age, a year was a remarkably short period of time. He could already see himself back in Garrett County while Krista remained here, and the ache he felt convinced him he was right to hold back with her. If he could hardly stand the thought of leaving her now, imagine how much worse it would be at the end of a year.

Yes, he must always keep that end in sight, he told himself firmly, even as his arms tightened around Krista. He would enjoy what they had while they had it. Yes, he silently insisted. He could handle it.

Krista lay quietly in Logan's arms, fairly bursting with the need to talk, to tell him how much she loved him, to savor and discuss every single moment of their magical, marvelous newfound intimacy. She felt so close to him, and ironically it was this closeness that kept her from pouring out all the love and joy she felt. Instinctively she sensed that an inner part of him remained reserved and aloof. Despite the passion they had shared, he was holding back. The emotional barrier she'd sensed earlier was still intact because he was deliberately keeping himself at an emotional distance.

Why? she wondered, and guessed the answers almost at once. He didn't trust her, he didn't love her.

Amy Sue might be out of the picture, but he still didn't want a high-earning professional woman, except in bed. It all came back to that. He wanted a sexual relationship with her. Period. He didn't want a lasting commitment or involvement. Hadn't he told her point-blank that their relationship was not going to be permanent?

She felt him shift and snuggled closer. He kissed her tenderly, lingeringly, then carefully eased her out of his arms and tucked the covers around her. "Go to sleep, sweetheart," he murmured softly. "Much as I hate to go, I'm afraid that I have to. I can't leave the kids alone all night."

"I know." She watched him dress. "And I understand." She threw back the covers and climbed out of bed. "I'll come downstairs with you."

"Honey, you don't have to. Stay in bed."

But Krista had already snatched her robe from its hook on the back of the bathroom door and was belting it around her. "I have something to give you," she said, a smile playing about her lips.

They walked downstairs together, their arms around each other. Krista hurried into the living room and removed a 45-rpm record from its case. "This is for you." She handed the record to Logan. "For your collection."

He stared at the disc. " 'Believe Me' by the Royal Teens? Krista, I can't take this record. It's valuable— and it was Eric's!"

"I want you to have it. You need it for your collection. And I'm sure that Eric would like the idea of a true connoisseur owning it. Who else could fully appreciate it?" She smiled up at him.

"I've been looking for this record for years." he stared at it, then at Krista. Her eyes were glowing like polished jewels. She wanted him to have it. She wished he had something to give her . . . She seemed to be forever giving to him and the children. But what could he give to a woman who could buy whatever she wanted for herself?

He took her in his arms. "Thank you, Krista. I'll think of you every time I play it. Believe me."

She groaned at his play on words. "Good night, Logan."

"Good night, Krista." They gazed into each other's eyes for a long moment, then Logan commanded gruffly, "Make sure you lock this door."

"I will." She opened the door for him and he stepped out into the night.

Logan listened for the sound of the key turning in the lock before he departed, clutching the prized old record in his hand.

Ten

"Krista!"

She turned at the sound of her name and saw Ross Perry hurrying across the courthouse parking lot toward her. "Hello, Ross. I haven't seen you for a while."

"You'll be seeing more of me than you want next week." He grimaced. "The Landau custody case."

Krista sighed. "I had all three of them—Gary, Marcia, and little Julie—in my office last week. Gary and Marcia started in on each other and poor Julie ran and hid under my desk. I had to threaten to call security to break up the brawl."

"I had a similar scene in my office." Ross shook his head. "That poor kid. She's starting to come unglued from all the hostility."

"At least she knows that although her parents hate each other, they both want her more than anything else in the world." Krista thought of the sad-eyed, anxious child and felt a pang of apprehension. "Julie seems to derive some comfort from that fact."

"It's all she has," Ross said. "This is one case I'll be glad to see come to trial and get settled. Unlike the Gladbury case . . ."

Krista smiled. "Lynette Gladbury and I are in no hurry to do anything at all."

"I know, I know, the old stalling strategy. You keep putting off the settlement discussion, knowing full well that Joel Gladbury, like almost every client, wants this case to be settled, not tried in court. And every day you refuse to meet, his insecurity builds." Ross gave her a half-admiring, half-annoyed smile. "I've used the same tactics myself."

"Tell Joel Gladbury that Lynette and I have no problem with going to trial. None at all."

"If I tell him that, he'll freak for sure. He's enhanced your courtroom abilities to mythological proportions."

She laughed. "I'll try hard to live up to it. I was on my way to lunch, Ross. Care to join me?"

"Sure. Are you buying?"

"Definitely. I can write it off as a business lunch. After all, we've discussed the Landaus and the Gladburys." She climbed into her car and unlocked the door for Ross. He settled himself in the seat beside her, then stared at her curiously.

"Do you mind if we discuss judges?" he asked. "A certain judge, that is. Logan Moore."

Krista pulled out of the parking lot and into the stream of traffic. "What about Logan?"

"There's a rumor going around the courthouse that he's disqualified himself from hearing any of your cases."

"Oh?" Krista studied the brilliant red of the traffic light as the car idled at an intersection. Logan hadn't told her he was going to do that, although it didn't surprise her that he had. He was every inch an ethical, conscientious, and professional officer of the court who wouldn't condone a lawyer presenting a case before a judge she'd been sleeping with for the past month.

Krista didn't condone it either and had been prepared to seek a change of venue had she been assigned to Logan's courtroom. Fortunately, she hadn't had to face the prospect. Her cases had been assigned to other judges this past month. Now she knew it wasn't just by chance.

"Naturally," Ross said, "that rumor has led to much juicy speculation about why Judge Moore feels he and Krista Conway can't be in the same courtroom together." Ross continued to regard her speculatively. "Care to comment?"

Krista steered the Bentley into the crowded parking lot of The Blue Goose, a small restaurant popular with the courthouse crowd because of its proximity to the building as well as its excellent sandwiches. "What type of comments have you been hearing?" she asked.

"Never give a straight answer when you can get by with another question, eh, Conway? Typical attorney!" Ross chuckled. "You're not on the stand, Krista. I'm only asking to satisfy my own admittedly intense curiousity. And my wife's. Calla says she sees the Moore kids at your place all the time. She's even seen the boy driving your Bentley. What gives?"

A waiter seated them at a booth and handed each a menu. "Logan and I are very, very good friends," Krista said.

"Mmm-hmm."

"And the children are my friends, too."

Ross's smile widened. "Is it too soon for Calla and me to plan your farewell party? I can't tell you how happy it makes me to think of you practicing in Garrett County while I take over your title as premier bomber in the area. Perhaps you'll be kind enough to pass my name along to all your clients, old and new? Never know when one will need a good divorce lawyer, hmm?"

"Who said I was leaving? And why would I set up a practice in Garrett County?" Krista asked lightly, even though her heart felt heavy in her chest. Ross assumed she was going to marry Logan and move back to Garrett County with him. "Sorry to dash your hopes, Ross, but I'm firmly entrenched here."

But she would leave in a minute, if Logan asked her to, she admitted bleakly to herself. If she'd been in love with Logan that first night she slept with him, her emotions had deepened irrevocably and increased a thousandfold during this past month with him.

They were together most of their nonworking hours. Somehow, she had taken over the responsibility of dinner for the Moore family. Denise had completely opted out. She hated to cook, probably because she'd been thrust into the job at such a young age due to her mother's illness and death.

It had seemed natural for Krista to step in when Denise called and asked for help in the kitchen, and even more so when Denise became more involved in after-school activities and didn't have time to prepare a meal. There would be nothing for dinner when Logan came home, and he and all three children would be hungry. Krista couldn't let them live their lives eating hamburgers and pizza. She began planning, shopping, and cooking for the family. Dinner at Krista's quickly became an established daily routine.

It seemed perfectly natural anyway, because the children were always at her house. Denise and her friends didn't want to watch *Guiding Light* on any other television but Krista's big new set. And Mitch's record albums only sounded right on Krista's new stereo system. Krista gave them a key and they went directly to her house after school. Lauren was always there too, of course. She played with the cats and her Barbie dolls, many of whom had taken up permanent residence in the spare bedroom.

After dinner Krista was still with the Moores. The kids did their homework at her kitchen table while she cleaned up the kitchen and Logan watched the news on TV. She helped Lauren with her homework, and later she and Logan and the kids watched television or listened to music or read in companionable silence. On weekend afternoons, Krista and Logan took the children to see the many sites of interest in and around Washington, D.C.

When the Moores went home for the night, her house seemed deserted and empty. Even Tao and Ink noticed and prowled through the rooms, meowing as they looked for Lauren.

And inevitably, every night between ten-thirty and eleven o'clock, Logan would return to knock on her door. Her heart racing, she would fly to open it, and he would take her into his arms and . . . Krista flushed. She quickly snapped out of her reverie to find Ross Perry watching her with amused speculation.

"You're wearing the same look my daughter does when she gazes at Don Johnson on TV," he said, grinning. "And you're thinking of Logan Moore. Firmly entrenched, Krista? I don't think so. My hopes aren't at all dashed. Your days as a Montgomery County lawyer are drawing to a close whether you admit it or not."

She ought to deny it strenuously, Krista thought. She didn't, though, because she wished so much it were true. Sadly for her, it wasn't. Logan had no intention of marrying her. He enjoyed her company and her friendship with his children and he enjoyed her in bed. But he didn't love her. She knew it because she was so in love with him, and therein lay the contrast.

When they made love, she gave everything she had to give, her body, her soul, her heart and mind. She was his and she let him know it in every way. She couldn't hold back. She was too much in love even to want to try.

But Logan, despite his passion and ardor, had never dismantled the emotional barrier he'd erected between them. Since their very first night together when she had sensed he was deliberately controlling his response to her, she had known he didn't belong to her. He gave her much pleasure in bed, gave her his companionship out of bed, but he didn't give himself to her. He had no intention of making their relationship a permanent one.

He didn't love her. She was too different from the type of woman he thought he wanted. It hurt, but Krista tried not to dwell on it. Eric's death had taught her to live in the present, to make the most of each day while she was living it. She loved Logan, and for now, for a while, they were together. For now, for a while, the five of them were almost like a real family. Krista didn't dare ask for any more than that.

"Daddy, it was the best Halloween party ever!" Lauren cried excitedly when Logan walked into Krista's kitchen one evening later that week. "We had cupcakes and cookies and soda and lots of candy and we bobbed for apples!" She danced around the kitchen as she talked. "Everyone loved my costume and Krissy bought everyone in the class two packages of monster bubble-gum cards, and can I go trick-or-treating tonight with Holly Wilson? Please!"

Krista watched Lauren with amusement. "Holly Wilson is Lauren's best friend in her class," she explained to Logan. "I met her mother today when she came to pick up Holly at school this afternoon."

"And Holly is coming over here tomorrow after school," Lauren added. "Her mother said it's okay. Oh, I have to get Denise to put more green in my hair. Bye!" She raced from the kitchen.

"Did I just see a whirlwind streak by?" Logan asked. "One with a blue, green, and orange ponytail?" He smiled. "I didn't have the heart to ask Lauren exactly what her costume is. She looks like something from out of the twilight zone. Or the circus."

"She's a punk rocker," Krista informed him. "As was every other girl in her class. So were most of the boys—the ones who weren't wearing camouflage clothing, that is. They looked like guerrilla soldiers."

Logan wrapped his arms around her waist and pulled her back against him. "A far cry from when we were kids and everybody dressed as witches and clowns and hoboes." He nibbled on her sensitive neck and Krista felt her pulses leap in immediate response to his caresses.

"I had a chance to view Halloween from a teacher's perspective today," she said. Her eyelids fluttered as his hands slowly moved along her rib cage to settle just below her breasts. "Miss Dickson is an extraordinarily brave and calm woman. She didn't even blow her cool when a little boy named Albert nearly drowned himself bobbing for apples."

"I've often thought that teachers deserve hazardous-duty pay." Logan turned her in his arms and kissed her forehead, her cheeks, the tip of her nose. "So . . . do you still want to go through with this room-mother bit for the next two parties?"

"Of course. I've already promised Lauren. And it was fun—in a wild and manic sort of way." She smiled up at him. "I like the teacher, Miss Dickson, very much. She had some lovely things to say about Lauren."

There was one small problem, though, Krista thought. When she had told Miss Dickson on the class museum trip that her name was Ms. Conway, she had assumed she'd clarified her marital status and nonfamilial relationship to Lauren. Apparently she hadn't. Today, Miss Dickson had made it clear that she thought Ms. Conway was divorced from Lauren's father and had elected to use her maiden name. Miss Dickson believed she was Lauren's mother.

"Nowadays," she told Krista, "we have families that have different surnames for each member." And as Lauren had called her "Mom" all during the party, Miss Dickson's misconception had been virtually verified.

She ought to have corrected Lauren, Krista scolded herself. But she hadn't. Lauren seemed so thrilled to have her there, so proud to be "the room mother's child." And most of all, she'd *liked* hearing Lauren call her Mom. She wished she really were the little girl's mother.

The oven timer buzzed, and Krista left Logan's arms to remove the stuffed pork chops from the oven. "Oh, about Lauren playing with Holly Wilson tomorrow," she said. "I have to pick them up at school since Holly can't ride Lauren's bus. There's some regulation against kids riding any other bus but their assigned one. I'll bring them here and Holly's mother will pick her up at six."

Logan watched her heap the pork chops on a serving platter. "You'll have to leave your office early again," he said. Something she'd taken to doing at least once a week, he added silently, for reasons always involving the kids. Her flexible office hours were quite convenient, he acknowledged. She could leave whenever she wanted, something he was unable to do at the courthouse.

"I have to draw up the final draft of a prenuptial agreement for a client who's about to embark on his third marriage," she said. "I can do it here at home and have Vicky type it up the following day."

"Prenuptial agreement?" Logan arched his brows.

"Mmm. I handled this client's previous divorce, which was a tangled financial horror, and I told him at the time that if he ever married again—and I knew he would because he's the marrying kind—he should come to me for a prenuptial agreement beforehand. Thankfully, he took my advice." She placed the vegetables and salad on the table, along with the platter of meat.

"I realize that these prenuptial contracts are quite the current trend," Logan said, his expression thoughtful as he gazed at her.

She nodded. "I recommend them in certain circumstances—when one party is much wealthier than the other, or there are children from a previous marriage whose interests need to be protected. And for people who have already gone through a messy divorce."

"You would insist upon such a contract for yourself, of course."

Krista stared into space. "No, I wouldn't," she said slowly, for it was an idea she had considered carefully over the years. "I'd want marriage based on the kind of trust that didn't require a written contract." She smiled wistfully. "I suppose that sounds totally incongruous in view of my professional advice."

"Totally," he agreed. Another paradox that was Krista, he thought as he watched her swift, efficient movements around the kitchen. But her income clearly put her in the ranks of those who *should* consider a premarital agreement. And she was so generous and giving that she would foolishly want to share everything of hers with her mate. Her mate. He froze at the thought. For one horror-stricken minute he imagined her married to another man, sharing her love and laughter with him, sharing his bed . . .

The pain was so intense, he felt as if he'd been punched in the stomach. *She's mine!* he wanted to shout, even as a taunting little voice inside his head added cruelly, "Temporarily." This time next year he would be back in Garrett County and Krista would be here. Cooking dinner for another man? Anticipating their evening, and the long, long night, together? He caught his breath and swallowed hard. Every fiber in his being protested against such a picture.

Krista called the children for dinner, and Denise and Lauren arrived in the kitchen within seconds. "Mitch is on the phone," Denise announced.

Krista smiled. "It must be an important call to make him late for dinner." Mitch never missed a meal. He had the incredible appetite of a fast-growing teenage boy and consumed more food in one day than she ate in three.

"Oh, it's an important call, for sure," Denise said. "He's talking to Janna Nimick. One of her friends told one of his friends that Janna wanted to go to the dance with him this Friday. He finally worked up enough courage to call her."

"Who's Janna Nimick?" asked Logan.

"Janna's a cheerleader and she's really cute and popular," Denise said, grinning mischievously. "And she didn't know Mitch was alive until he gave her and her girlfriends a ride home from the Pizza Hut in Krista's Bentley two nights ago. That did it for Janna."

Mitch joined them at the table a moment later, looking somewhat dazed. "Janna said she'll go to the dance with me on Friday." He stumbled into his seat. "Janna Nimick with *me*!"

"You'd better ask Krista to let you borrow the Bentley," Lauren said

"There's no reason for Mitch to borrow Krista's car," Logan said firmly. "I'm perfectly willing to let you drive my car to the dance, son."

"Dad, I can't take Janna Nimick anywhere in that old heap." Mitch looked appalled. "A goddess doesn't ride in an old brown Dodge!"

"Certainly not," Krista said. She tried hard to suppress her laughter and managed to succeed. "I insist that you take the Bentley, Mitch."

"Thanks, Krista." He looked profoundly relieved. "Thank heavens *you* understand!"

"A goddess!" Logan shook his head, amused in spite of himself. His eyes met Krista's and they exchanged indulgent, adult smiles.

Now, thought Krista, ask him now. "Logan, I've been invited to a party at the Burning Tree Country Club this Saturday night and I wondered if you'd care to go with me." She realized she was holding her breath. She'd received the invitation two weeks ago and hadn't found the right moment to tell Logan about it. She knew he wouldn't want to go. He'd made it plain that he was a confirmed homebody who wouldn't appreciate an evening socializing with strangers.

She was right. He shifted in his chair and frowned. "I don't think that'll be possible, Krista. Denise and Mitch probably have plans and I'll have to stay with Lauren."

"I don't have any plans," Denise said quickly. "I'll stay with Lauren."

"A party, huh?" Mitch said. "Sounds good."

"Parties are fun. You'll have a good time, Daddy," Lauren added.

Logan looked at Krista. She silently acknowledged that it hadn't been fair of her to bring up the party with her three staunchest allies present. On the other hand . . . "I have to make an appearance at this party for business reasons, Logan." She didn't want to go alone, she wanted to be with him. "We don't have to stay long."

"Krista, I'm simply not interested in the area social scene. A big crush at some swank country club doesn't appeal to me in the slightest." He resumed eating. Apparently, as far as he was concerned, the discussion was over.

The children thought otherwise. "C'mon, Dad," Mitch said. "You can go to one party with Krista. You two never go anywhere. You spend every night at home. You're not *that* old!"

"You went to parties with Awful Amy Sue," Lauren reminded him.

"If Krista has to go to the party," Denise said, "she might have to get another date. You don't want her to go with Glen Fremont, do you, Dad?"

"Glen Fremont?" Krista repeated, staring at Denise. "The columnist for the *Post*?" She had met him a year ago and they'd dated infrequently since then. "How do you know him, Denise?"

"Oh, didn't I mention it?" Denise strove to look casual. "He . . . uh, called you. I guess I forgot to tell you."

"I guess you did." Krista said dryly. "Was I supposed to call him back?"

"As soon as you get back from Europe," Lauren said.

"Europe?" Krista, Logan, and Mitch chorused.

Denise stood up. "I think I'll skip dessert tonight. I have so much algebra homework, I'd better get started on it right away."

"Sit down, Denise," Logan ordered. She obeyed. "Now kindly explain the circumstances of this telephone call."

Denise sighed. "This Glen Fremont guy called last week and thought I was the maid or something. He said he wanted to talk to Krista about going to some party with him. So I . . . um, I said that Krista was in Europe. He said for her to give him a call when she got back."

Mitch laughed. "Way to go, Denise."

"Denise, that was outrageous, inexcusable interference," Logan said severely. "Not to mention a blatant lie. You owe Krista an apology. And I don't want you using the telephone for three days, so you'll have plenty of time to consider your actions."

"Three days without the phone?" Denise looked aghast at the prospect.

Lauren leaped to her sister's defense. "But Daddy, Denise had to tell him that! You didn't want Krissy to go to the party with somebody else, did you?"

"Krista is an adult who has the right to make her own decisions," Logan said. "And to receive her own telephone messages."

"You're right, Daddy. I'm sorry, Krista," Denise said sweetly, glancing from her father to Krista. "If you want, I'll call Mr. Fremont right now and tell him what I did and that you'll go to the party with him on Saturday night."

"No!" Logan stood up. "There's no need for that, Denise. I . . . er, I'm going to take Krista to the damn party."

"Daddy, you used a bad word!" Lauren scolded. "Swearing isn't nice."

"Manipulating people isn't nice either, Lauren." Logan shot Krista a glare. An I'll-talk-to-you-about-this-later glare.

Wisely, Mitch stepped in to change the subject completely.

The party wasn't mentioned again until later that evening, after the children had gone home, when Logan made his usual appearance at Krista's door at eleven P.M. She opened the door to let him in, but this time he didn't sweep her into his arms and kiss her as if he were starving for the taste and touch of her.

He stood in the small foyer and glowered at her. "I don't like the way you conspired with Denise to manipulate me into attending this party with you."

"I didn't conspire with Denise!" Krista said hotly. "She was manipulating your social life long before I appeared on the scene. Now it seems she's taken to managing mine, too."

"Denise shouldn't have intercepted your phone call and lied to the man," Logan conceded. "On the other hand, why are you getting phone calls from other men?" His tone was accusatory and Krista immediately took offense.

"Maybe because I'm a single woman, and Glen assumed I wasn't involved with anyone. It would be an easy mistake for him to make. You and I have never made any public acknowledgment of our relationship. There's been some gossip at the courthouse, but nothing else to link us together."

She paused to take a breath, and suddenly the words just poured out. "You don't want to meet my friends. I've turned down invitations from them to dinner or parties or the movies because you didn't want to go with them. I didn't mind because I wanted to be alone with you, but I—I'm beginning to see things differently. The reason you didn't want to be with my friends has nothing to do with your wanting to be alone with me. You just don't want to bother with the social side of a—a strictly temporary relationship."

Logan's jaws tightened. He could have told her that he'd deliberately kept away from her friends—and in turn, kept her from them—because he was hoping to wean her away from them, to lessen the importance in her life of anyone here in Montgomery County. He had a lot of friends back home in Garrett County. He knew they would like Krista and she would like them. They could have as active a social life there as she wished. If she came back with him . . .

But she wasn't coming back with him. They had only a temporary relationship. In case he was in danger of forgetting that, Krista had just reminded him. So Logan said nothing, nothing at all.

Krista stared at him. His eyes were hard, his expression implacable. He hadn't denied what she'd said, thus . . . confirming it? She was a convenience to Logan. She cooked for him and slept with him. Temporarily. Her eyes filled with angry tears. How had she landed herself in such a position?

Logan ran his hand through his dark hair, tousling it. "I told you I'd go to the party with you." His fingers caught and encircled her wrist. "Let's go upstairs."

She gaped at him. "And make love? Now?"

"Yes."

"We're in the middle of a quarrel and you expect me to hop into bed with you? Just like that?" Krista was incensed.

"I don't know what we're quarreling about. I told you I'd take you to the damn party. You've gotten what you wanted."

"And now I should give you what *you* want. Is that the point you're trying to make?"

He dropped her wrist. "I was under the impression you wanted it, too."

She shook her head. "Not now."

He stared at her. "So the Modern and Independent Woman is resorting to the oldest female trick in the book. Withholding sex as a punishment."

"I am not withholding sex! I just don't feel like making love when I'm infuriated."

"I'm not going to beg for milady's favors," he said in clipped tones. "If you want me to leave, just say the words."

She wanted to scream with fury and frustration. The situation—and her position—was completely untenable. She was deeply in love with a man who didn't love her. She wanted permanence with all its inherent problems, he wanted temporary convenience. How long could she hold on to her self-respect under such circumstances? Krista was certain of one thing, though . . . "If we go to bed tonight, we won't be making love, Logan. We'll simply be having sex."

"More semantics, counselor?" He managed a thin smile. "If I wanted to play word games, I'd do the crossword puzzle in the newspaper."

"I'm not playing games." Her voice was shaking and she knew she was perilously close to tears. She couldn't stand the thought of crying in front of Logan. He would probably feel sorry for her, but it wouldn't change his feelings. He didn't love her. She'd known that and had thought she could cope with it. But she couldn't, she simply couldn't. "You said just to say the words, so I'll say them. I want you to leave, Logan."

He wanted to refuse. All his atavistic male instincts rose to the fore, and it took every ounce of his civilized control not to throw her over his shoulder and carry her upstairs, to make love to her until she knew beyond a question of a doubt that she belonged to him. To tell her so and make her repeat it after him until she would never forget. There was nothing temporary about his feelings for her. They were together forever.

But a judicious and self-controlled man didn't resort to such primitive tactics. He'd known all along that his relationship with Krista was a temporary one. He'd thought—hoped—it would last the year he was here, but he'd always known it wasn't permanent between them. And he'd convinced himself that he could handle it. He *could* handle it! He would handle it now.

"If I leave now, I won't be coming back," he said tersely.

Krista's heart plummeted. More than anything, she wanted to ask him to stay, to throw herself into his arms and lose herself in their impassioned lovemaking. But she didn't. She'd thought she could cope with the restrictions he'd put on their relationship, but she couldn't accept his limited, temporary terms any longer. Loving him, she couldn't stay with him knowing that he didn't intended it to last.

She held her head high and said nothing.

"I don't want an on-again, off-again affair," he said. He tried to read her expression, but he couldn't. She wore a mask he couldn't interpret. "If I walk out that door, it's over."

He expected her to call his bluff; he prayed that she would. But she didn't.

He had no choice, did he? Logan turned and wordlessly walked out the door.

Eleven

Breaking up was harder to do when there were children involved. Krista had been made well aware of that fact from her divorce practice, but she'd certainly never expected to experience it in her own life.

Mitch, Denise, and Lauren weren't about to disappear merely because their father had told them he'd had an argument with Krista. They chose to ignore totally that fact. If anything, they spent *more* time at her house. Lauren called her Mommy right in front of Logan. Mitch continued to borrow her car. None of them left for home at dinnertime, and Krista found herself cooking meals as usual, at least for the children. She didn't ask about Logan, but Denise volunteered the information, anyway. "Dad's been having TV dinners at home. We told him we'd rather eat here with you."

On Saturday, Krista took the children to a nearby shopping mall where the kids browsed while she hurriedly chose a black cocktail dress to wear to the party that night. She made it home in time to shower and dress, and was in the middle of putting on her makeup when the telephone rang. It was Mitch and he sounded frantic. "Krista, you've got to come quick! It's Lauren. She's sick!"

"Is she rolling around on the floor holding her stomach and screaming in agony?" Krista asked.

"Not this time. She's got a fever—a high one! A hundred and six. Denise just took her temperature."

Krista didn't miss a beat. "May I speak to Denise, please?"

Denise got on the line. "Krista, you've got to come! Did Mitch tell you about Lauren's fever?"

"Yes, he did. You stuck the thermometer in boiling water, I presume."

There was a long silence.

"Denise?"

"How did you know?" Denise asked glumly.

"The temperature was too high. And it came on too fast. I just saw Lauren less than an hour ago and she was fine, remember?"

"We don't want you to go to that party!" Denise wailed. "What if you meet a man and fall in love with him?"

Krista could have told the girl that was impossible. She was already in love and no man at any party could erase Logan from her heart. But why encourage false hopes in either of them? "Denise, I'm going to the party," she said quietly.

"Daddy doesn't want you to go, either. He's in a terrible mood! He—"

"Honey, I know it's difficult for you, but your father and I are—"

"No, don't say it!" Denise interrupted. "I have to go clean my room now. I'd rather do anything than hear you say—*that*!" She hung up before Krista could get in another word.

As it happened, Krista did meet another man at the party. Or re-met one—Jeremy Litman, the Justice Department attorney whose attempt to take her to dinner had been sabotaged by Denise and Lauren.

The girls had admitted it to her one afternoon, and Krista, lost in love with Logan, had merely laughed off their intervention.

Tonight Jeremy himself was in the mood to laugh about their missed connection and to apologize for his earlier bad temper. "I'm not usually so impatient and rude," he explained sheepishly, "but my apartment had been burglarized two days before and the frustration of not being able to get in touch with you was the finishing touch to a truly terrible week."

Krista instantly sympathized with him and told him about her own burglary. Their rapport was immediate. Jeremy didn't leave her side for the rest of the evening. Krista enjoyed his company. He was attentive and witty, and did not hold her career against her. On the contrary, he was openly admiring of her prowess and success. Krista talked and laughed and, to her great despair, she missed Logan more than ever.

"Let's escape from this mob and go someplace quiet for a drink," Jeremy suggested when their conversation was interrupted by other guests for the tenth or twelfth time.

Krista was about to refuse automatically, but he didn't give her the chance. "I know a great little place in Southwest Washington. You can follow me there in your car and then I'll follow you home later."

"I really don't—" she began, but he interrupted her again.

"I'm not going to try to force my way inside your house tonight. I just want to make sure you get safely home. We've both been recent victims of burglaries, remember? I'll leave you at your doorstep, I promise." He was very persuasive and Krista really didn't want to go home to her empty house and the sleepless, lonely night she knew was in store for her.

She agreed to Jeremy's plans.

·　·　·

He hadn't thought she would actually go to the party without him, Logan admitted to himself as he walked past Krista's house at ten o'clock that night. He'd tried to call her earlier. When he reached the recorded message on her answering machine, he'd walked the two blocks to her house and peered inside her garage. The Bentley wasn't there. She'd gone to the party, after all. Alone or with a date? he wondered as he stared into the empty garage.

Probably alone, he decided, trying to console himself. She'd driven her own car, hadn't she? Or did these cool urban men not mind having a woman pick them up and drive? Logan imagined Krista arriving at the exclusive country club with some debonair city slicker—the type who owned his own tux—and his stomach began to churn.

He'd missed her so much this week, he knew he couldn't go on this way. It was time to put his pride aside, to put his heart on the line, and try to convince her to drop her notions of a temporary affair. He would tell her he loved her and wanted her in his life permanently. He would try to persuade her to leave her fabulous career behind and move back to Garrett County with him when his year as visiting judge was over.

She could practice law in Garrett County, couldn't she? Of course, she would never make the kind of money she made here. . . . Logan's palms began to sweat. Was he a hopeless fool to expect a woman like Krista to leave behind a high income and an established, successful law practice to become the wife of a mountain-county judge? To become an instant mother of three?

He paced the sidewalk in front of her home. When was she going to come home? He had to talk to her tonight. Finally, after twenty more minutes of pacing, Logan decided to go home and come back a little later.

He called her house at eleven o'clock and every

fifteen minutes thereafter, but he got the answering machine every time. He didn't bother to leave a message. Dammit, where was she? he wondered. He was torn by a nerve-wracking combination of frustration, anxiety, and anger, the emotions so mixed that he couldn't begin to sort one from the other.

He tried to distract himself by watching television, and when that failed he took out his treasured collection of rock and roll records. He played "Tragedy," "Mr. Blue," and "Going Out of My Head," and felt as if he were living all three. He listened to only the opening bars of "Believe Me" and had to turn it off. It reminded him painfully of Krista. His attempt at a musical diversion was a dismal failure.

At one-thirty, he was back on the street, heading for Krista's house once more. Where in the hell was she? he fumed. He felt as charged as a lightning rod. If she didn't come back soon . . .

He cursed at the sight of the empty garage. What was he going to do now? Should he assume she'd been in an accident and begin dialing area hospitals? That actually sounded preferable to the alternate assumption—that Krista was spending the night with another man.

He had turned to return to his home when he spied the headlights of two cars approaching Krista's house. He recognized the make of one of the cars at once. It was a Bentley. His heart hammered in his chest as he quickly slipped to the side of the house and concealed himself in the hedge.

This was, Logan decided grimly, definitely one of the low points of his life. Hiding in the bushes in the middle of the night and spying on a woman—who was talking and laughing quite happily with another man!

The man had pulled his sporty red Corvette into the driveway behind Krista's car and was walking her to her door, his arm around her waist. Jeal-

ousy, the force of which he'd never known, seared
Logan like a blade of fire.

Krista was wearing a short, strapless black dress
and high-heeled black shoes. She looked sexy and
sophisticated and expensive. And she'd never seemed
further out of his reach than she did at this moment, walking to her door with that elegantly dressed
yuppie whose intimidatingly expensive sports car
was idling in her driveway.

Logan watched the two of them pause to chat for a
few minutes at her door. His body went rigid with
pain and shock when the man bent his head and
brushed his lips against Krista's. The kiss—if it
could even be called that, it was so fleeting—lasted
all of a second. But to Logan, it seemed to go on
forever.

Then Krista went inside her house and the man
dashed to his Corvette and was gone. Logan stood
in the darkness as the pain drained from him and
was replaced by a ferocious anger. For the first time
in his life he couldn't seem to think through a situation. He could only act. On a purely emotional im-
pulse, he marched to the front door and pounded on
it.

Krista opened it almost at once. When she saw
Logan towering before her, her jaw dropped open.
"Logan!" she managed shakily, and her astonishment turned swiftly into a burst of joy. Logan was
here! She'd missed him so much, and now, as if in
answer to her prayers and dreams, he'd come back
to her!

But Logan was blind to the radiance of Krista's
face and the glow in her eyes. Or if he saw them, he
didn't attribute them to his presence but to her
escort's kiss. He pushed his way inside the house,
clenching his hands into fists and jamming them
into his pockets. It seemed like an effective way to
prevent himself from touching her. For if he touched
her . . .

Krista was suddenly aware of the terrible tension emanating from Logan. She didn't realize it was anger. Yet. "Is something wrong?" she asked. "Has something happened to one of the children?" Her heart pounded at the thought.

Logan stared at the creamy swell of her breasts, so tantalizingly displayed by the bodice of the strapless dress. His gaze lowered to the curves of her waist and hips, and then to the short, flirty skirt that enhanced the long shapeliness of her legs.

"You little witch!" he rasped.

Krista paled.

"Logan, I—"

"I saw you and your new boyfriend necking on the porch. Were you hoping I was him and that I'd changed my mind and come back to bed you after all?"

"No!" she said breathlessly. "I—"

"You went to that party tonight," he interrupted, his tone furiously accusing, "with the express purpose of picking up a man. And you did it, you trashy little—"

Krista didn't let him finish. Acting on pure instinct, she drew back her hand and slapped his cheek with her palm, hard. The resounding crack seemed to echo in the sudden, stunned silence.

For what felt like forever, neither moved, spoke, or breathed. Then simultaneously they lunged at each other and kissed and kissed until both were panting and gasping for breath. Hands stroked and caressed urgently, desperately, fueling the raging fires that blazed between them.

They didn't even make it up the stairs. Hastily discarded clothes were strewn from the hall into the living room, where Krista and Logan sank onto the long blue sofa.

They whirled together in a consuming, overwhelming maelstrom of passion, oblivious to everything and anything but their indomitable need for each other. He was strong and hard and smooth. Velvet steel. She was creamy soft, tightly sheathing him as they both groaned with pleasure.

Krista gave herself to him completely as she always did, without reservation or restraint. But this time she took even as she gave, demanded even as she surrendered. Logan felt the reins of his control slipping away as he was drawn deeper and deeper into her. She gazed into his glittering black eyes, felt him tremble in her arms, and knew that he was as vulnerable as she.

They moved together in sensual rhythm, in hotly erotic tandem, and the shimmering, shivering pleasure built and grew to a shattering intensity. Then the sweet flames engulfed them and they exploded into a tumultuous, simultaneous climax.

Krista clutched Logan's shoulders and tears of joy stained her cheeks. This time, for the first time, Logan had not held back. They had shared passion before, but this was more than passion. It was deeper, stronger, a mystical union of their bodies and souls. Logan had given up his iron-willed self-control and lost himself in the deep, timeless strength of their love.

He loved her, her heart proclaimed exultantly. A man like Logan couldn't let go and merge so totally and completely with a woman unless he was deeply in love. She clung to him, crying softly, as happiness rolled over her.

Slowly, reluctantly Logan returned to earth from the rapturous plane to which he had ascended. He opened his eyes and raised himself up on his elbows so he could gaze down at Krista. She was crying!

He jackknifed into a sitting position. Good Lord, what had he done? Torrid images ran through his mind like a filmstrip, but he viewed them from the perspective of Krista's tears. Suddenly, their mutual explosion of passion didn't seem so mutual.

He saw himself grabbing her in the hall, but failed

to remember that she'd grabbed him at the same time. He saw his mouth close fiercely over hers, but forgot that her lips had parted instantaneously for him and her tongue had slipped into his mouth.

His gaze flickered over the trail of clothing, and it was obvious to him that he'd almost torn off her clothes. It was less obvious that she'd done the same to his. He stared down at her body, glistening with perspiration, saw her sweat-damp hair and tear-streaked face, and felt sick. For the first time ever he'd ceded control of himself and his emotions, and the results horrified him. He'd turned into a wild man and had brutally taken Krista against her will! And on the sofa!

He felt decadent, debased. He had never made love on a sofa in the middle of a living room in his entire life. He'd never made love anywhere but on a bed placed properly and appropriately in the bedroom.

He stood up and hastily began to gather up his clothes and pull them on. "Krista, I don't know what to say." His voice was taut and low and very, very controlled. "I never meant for this to happen. It—it'll never happen again, I promise you that."

Krista sat up and stared at him. No, her mind screamed. It wasn't happening. Not now. Logan couldn't leave her after what had happened between them. She watched him dress, his expression grim and forbidding.

He was leaving *because* of what had happened between them, she realized bleakly. He felt trapped and threatened. He'd wanted a limited, controlled relationship, and tonight they'd gone beyond that. Tonight marked a dramatic change in their relationship, and he knew it and didn't want any part of it.

"I won't see you again," Logan continued, his voice harsh with self-recrimination. Something about Krista had touched off the explosive, sensual drives within him and caused him to go berserk. It wasn't her fault, of course. It was his. If he were to continue seeing her, he knew, much to his shame, that it would happen again . . .

"I'll try to keep the kids away," he added, and went cold at the thought. "As long as they're around you, I—" His voice broke off and he swallowed. He was tempted to use his own children as a way to see her, to have her. He was truly a man beyond redemption.

Krista tried to say something, but she couldn't speak or swallow. Her throat felt as if she'd swallowed a ball of ground glass. She slumped weakly against the sofa cushions, tears streaming down her cheeks, her shoulders shaking with silent sobs.

Logan's heart contracted at the sight. "Krista." He came to stand in front of her. He couldn't leave her like this. Awkwardly, he bent and placed his hand on her shoulder.

Krista flinched. The last thing she wanted was his sympathy. He'd told her he didn't want her, and was he now going to console her for her loss? A white-hot flash of rage spun through her. "Go away!" she whispered, her voice little more than a hoarse croak. "Leave me alone!"

Logan felt as if he'd been stabbed in the heart. Of course, it was nothing less than he deserved under the circumstances, but that didn't lessen his pain. He murmured something unintelligible and quickly strode from the room.

Krista heard the front door close and knew he was gone. She buried her face in her hands and wept.

Logan glanced at his watch and suppressed a groan. It was only eleven A.M. and all the songs ever recorded about the misery that was Monday couldn't compare to the way he was feeling this Monday morning. He hadn't slept a wink since leaving Krista, well over twenty-four hours ago.

Sunday had been interminable. He'd thought of nothing but Krista. In an effort to get away, he'd taken the kids for a prolonged tour of the Skyline

Drive, but though the autumn foliage was in its full splendor, he'd barely seen a leaf. He kept seeing Krista, small and naked and crying on the sofa as he'd left her. By the time they had arrived home, it had been time for the kids to go to bed.

Lauren had tried to call Krista then, only to get her answering machine. Logan had spent the rest of the evening and night thinking about Krista, worrying about her, berating himself for what he'd done to her. He'd raped her! The admission was an ugly one, but he forced himself to bear the guilt. What else could grabbing a woman and stripping her in the hall and then taking her on the sofa be called?

His head was throbbing, and Logan rubbed his temples, then looked at his watch again. He needed more coffee or he would never make it through the day. He went to the canteen in the basement of the courthouse building. It was almost deserted at this hour—too late for a mid-morning break and too early for lunch.

He spotted Judges Flynn and Wright sitting at one table, deeply engrossed in conversation. He decided not to join them. He wasn't fit company for anyone this morning, and the aggressive and caustic Candace Flynn never ceased to unnerve him.

When she caught sight of him and motioned him over, Logan knew it was going to be that kind of day. And he deserved whatever he got, he mentally chastened himself.

He joined the two judges at their table. "What in the hell have you done to Krista Conway, Moore?" Candy demanded. Logan was so shocked, he jerked and his coffee sloshed over the sides of the cup, scalding his hand.

Roger Wright solicitously produced napkins and offered them to him. Candy merely glared and repeated her question. Logan swallowed and stared, speechless.

"I've always had the utmost respect professionally

for Krista Conway," Candy went on, fuming, "although I questioned her judgment when she plunged into an affair with you, Moore. Nothing personal, of course, but it's sheer idiocy for an attorney to take up with a judge."

"Well, this affair has obviously taken its toll on her." Candy sighed heavily. "I suppose you heard what happened in my courtroom this morning? I imagine Conway ran weeping right into your arms."

Logan's brows drew together. "I've been in court all morning. I haven't heard a thing. What happened?" Every nerve, every muscle in his body was tense.

"The Landau case happened," Candy said with disgust. "And it turned into a debacle the likes of which I've never seen. It started out badly and went downhill from there. Neither Conway nor Perry had any control over their clients, a first for both of them, I think. Gary and Marcia Landau kept sniping at each other while they and all the other witnesses were on the stand. No one, not even me, could shut them up." She lit a cigarette and drew in deeply.

"Krista told me about the Landau case," Logan said. "Both parents were almost pathologically obsessed with gaining sole custody of their child."

"They're pathological, all right." Candy sniffed. "And they chose the damnedest moment to let it all out— when the bailiff was bringing their daughter into the courtroom to take the stand."

Logan stared. "What happened?"

"All hell broke lose," she said grimly. "Gary Landau suddenly stood up and screamed at Marcia, 'All right, I'll give you what you claim to want so much. You can have the expletive deleted kid.' And then Marcia comes back with, 'Oh, no, you're not sticking me with your expletive deleted brat. I only wanted her because you said you did. I'd do anything to make you miserable.' "

"And the child heard this?" Logan was appalled.

"Every word. Her father bellowing that he only wanted Julie 'to teach her bitch of a mother a lesson.' That he'd never wanted the kid from the moment she was born, that he didn't even think Julie *was* his kid. Naturally, Marcia was ready with her share of comebacks. The poor kid was devastated."

"Terrible." Roger Wright shook his head. "What did you do?"

"What could I do? First I slapped both *expletive deleted* parents with stiff contempt-of-court fines. Then I prepared to decide what to do with the child— place her in the temporary custody of her maternal grandmother. I was *not* prepared for one of my attorneys to become as unglued as the little kid." Candy cast an accusing glare at Logan. "Your girlfriend disgraced herself in court this morning, Moore. She was crying as hard as the girl. Conway ran over and picked up the child and the two of them sobbed while Gary and Marcia cursed each other out. I can't tell you what a disaster it was."

"Krista was crying?" Logan repeated tautly.

Candy scowled. "I was terribly disappointed in her."

"It's a very sad case," Roger said. "Watching that poor child witness her parents renouncing her would be damn hard to take."

"Of course it's sad," Candy said irritably. "But you can't get emotionally involved in cases. Ross Perry didn't cry. *I* didn't cry." She stood up and turned to Logan. "I suggest you tell your lover that I don't want to see her in my courtroom until she's turned herself back into a dispassionate attorney, Judge Moore."

Her head held high, Judge Flynn stalked grandly from the canteen. The two men watched her go.

"Whew!" Roger shook his head. "She's a tough one. Too bad Krista dared to exhibit signs of humanity in Candace Flynn's courtroom."

Logan stood up. Blood was pounding in his head. "I have to find Krista."

"Tell her not to worry. You can't be disbarred for shedding a few tears for an unfortunate child." Roger took another sip of his coffee. Logan was already halfway to the door.

He called Krista's office, and her secretary told him that Miss Conway had left for the day. She didn't know whether or not Miss Conway had gone home.

Logan prayed that she had. He had to see her. Thoughts tumbled through his head as he drove. Krista had cried in court. She'd been so touched by the child's misery that she had broken down in front of the dragon, Judge Flynn. He wanted to hold her, to comfort her. To tell her that he respected her capacity to become emotionally involved, to cry for an abandoned child.

He wanted to tell her that he loved her. If she would just give him another chance, he would never hurt her again . . .

The blue Bentley was parked in her driveway and Logan's heart leaped in anticipation at the sight of it. He rang the doorbell impatiently, once, twice, three times.

When she didn't immediately answer, he began to pound on the door and call her name. It was almost anticlimactic when she finally opened the door. Logan stared at her. He wasn't sure what he was expecting—a sobbing, hysterical woman, perhaps?—but Krista was calm and composed. She was wearing pale pink slacks and a pink sweater, and looked soft and feminine and irresistible.

"Logan," she said. Her voice trembled a little, but she betrayed no further sign of emotion.

"Candace Flynn told me what happened with the Landau case this morning," he said quickly, needing an opening. There was always the chance she would slam the door in his face.

She winced. "It was the worst case I've ever handled. I've been through some acrimonious divorces,

out none of my previous clients have consciously
and deliberately tried to destroy their own children."
She swallowed. "I should've seen it coming. I had
. . strange feelings about this case, but . . ."

"Candace Flynn said you cried in court."

Krista managed a slight smile. "She was totally
offended. She thinks I'm an overemotional twit who's
let down every female who ever passed the bar exam."

"I wish I'd been the judge in that case. I wouldn't
have condemned you for feeling that little girl's pain."
He touched his fingertips to her chin and tilted her
face upward, forcing her to meet his gaze. "You're a
compassionate and sensitive woman, Krista, and
knowing that makes what I've done to you all the
worse." He drew in a deep breath and threw all pride
and reserve to the wind. "Krista, can you ever forgive me for—for what happened on Saturday night?"

She stared at him. "Forgive you?"

"I don't know what happened to me that night,
Krista. I just seemed to snap. I lost—"

"That all-powerful control of yours," she finished
for him. "For the first time I felt as if you were
willing to let go and give to me what I need to give to
you. For the first time I felt as if you wanted to share
more than your body with me. That you wanted a
future with me rather than a temporary fling. You
smashed the emotional barrier between us at last
. . ." Her lips quivered for a second, but she quickly
regained control. "But then you said you regretted it
and that you didn't want to see me again. You don't
even want me to see your children anymore."

"But I—I practically raped you that night! I undressed you in the hall! I made love to you on the
sofa!"

Krista was totally nonplussed. "You thought that
was rape?" She remembered their frantic, passionate
coming together. She'd been as eager and demanding as he. A glimmer of hope began to penetrate the
darkness that had enshrouded her heart since the

night he left her. "Logan, I undressed you in the hall, I made love with you on the sofa. Are you accusing me of rape, too?"

"Krista, I lost my head. Completely!"

She linked her arms loosely around his neck. "It's about time. I lose my head every time you kiss me. Surely you know that."

"Well, yes." he admitted, "but it's supposed to be different for a man. He's supposed to be in charge, in control of himself at all times."

"Another one of your dumb macho ideas." She shook her head. "Why does a man have to be in charge all the time? Why can't a man give up his choking mantle of responsibility and control and just let go with the woman he—" She halted and searched his face.

"The woman he loves," he finished for her. "I do, you know. I love you, Krista. I love you so much that I tried to protect myself from the pain of losing you before it ever happened. You're right. I deliberately held back with you because I knew if I didn't . . ." He held her as if he never wanted to let her go. "Sweetheart, I can't lose you!"

"You're not going to lose me, Logan." Her eyes filled with tears. "Darling, I love you, too. How could you not know it?" She stood on tiptoe to kiss him, pressing her mouth firmly against his and slipping the tip of her tongue between his lips.

Logan's response was immediate and ardent. One of his hands went to the small of her back and arched her into the masculine cradle of his body while his other hand cupped the nape of her neck. The kiss deepened, becoming fervent and passionate. Both were trembling when they drew apart to catch their breath.

"I want to marry you," Logan said, "and I needn't tell you how much the kids want me to marry you." He gazed down into her sapphire-blue eyes and thought he'd never seen her look so beautiful. "Will

ou marry me, Krista? And be a family with the kids
nd me?"

She smiled and framed his face with her hands.
"Yes, Logan. I want to marry you—and the kids—
more than anything on earth."

"I'll resign from the bench in Garret County," he
said bravely. "I'll sell the house and we'll live here
permanently. I can practice law, or maybe get a
government job. You can continue with your career
and the kids and I will be behind you all the way."

"Oh, Logan!" She hugged him tight, loving him all
the more for the sacrifices he was willing to make
for her. But she wouldn't ask that of him. She loved
him too much to have him give up everything that
was important to him. He'd come so far in reshap-
ing his attitudes. The Logan Moore she'd first met
wouldn't have considered marriage to a full-time career woman who outearned him. But he loved her
enough to do so now.

"Logan, I don't want you to resign from the bench.
You're a fine judge and I wouldn't dream of asking
you to give that up for me. I'll go back to Garrett
County with you when the year is up. It's your home
and the kids' home, and I'm ready for a change. I felt
so empty in court this morning, my life seemed so
empty. I felt helpless, knowing there was nothing I
could do to help little Julie Landau."

Krista gazed up at him, her blue eyes earnest and
intent. "It occurred to me in that courtroom today
that I've presided over so many broken dreams, so
many shattered lives. Too many. I want something
else in my life, something more. I want to build
something that will last, to give more than legal
advice. I want to have more than a—a high income
and a high-powered career."

She swallowed. "I want to help raise your children, and I want to have your baby, Logan. And I'll
stay at home and be a full-time wife and mother if
you want me to."

She buried her face in his chest and cuddled close
His arms tightened around her and he nuzzled he
neck. He'd gotten what he wanted, he thought. Krist
was going to be his wife and have his babies an
stay at home, dependent on him, in the tradition
mode. So why wasn't he exulting in his triumph
Hadn't his fondest wish just been granted?

It had, but . . . He held Krista close and remen
bered the first time he'd seen her in the courtroon
He'd been impressed by her skills, by the quick agi
ity of her mind. She was an excellent attorney. She
studied all those years to become one and had bee
immensely successful in establishing a career. H
admired her for that.

It seemed like such a shame for her to give it a
up. And suddenly it seemed ridiculous to want t
change the woman he'd fallen so deeply in love with

Krista drew back a little and looked up at him. H
onyx eyes were thoughtful. She touched a finger t
his lips and traced them slowly, sensuously. "Yo
look like you're deciding a case, Your Honor. I'
seen you wear that same expression in the cour
room."

He caught her hand and kissed each fingertij
"It's finally occurred to me that it doesn't have to t
all-or-nothing in marriage, Krista. Those neat litt
categories I placed women in no longer seem to ap
ply." His smile was so warm and loving that Krist
felt pure joy ripple through her. "Neither of us ha
to sacrifice everything. Why don't we work out a
acceptable compromise, counselor?"

"A compromise?"

"Garrett County could use an attorney as skille
in family law as you are, sweetheart. I'll simply di
qualify myself from hearing any of your cases. You'
already proven how ably you can handle a caree
and family commitments. You've made time for tl
kids and juggled your office hours in ways that
never could."

"A part-time practice would be perfect," she said. "There's no reason why I couldn't work just a few days a week until the baby is older."

"Or babies," he added with a sexy smile. "I think I want at least two more children."

"Oh, do you?" she grinned. "Back to calling the shots, hmm?"

"I want whatever you want, darling," he said piously. "My consciousness has been well and truly raised."

She laughed. "What's the name of that Buddy Holly tune— 'That'll Be the Day'?" Her face was radiant with love. "I think I'd like to have two babies, too. And Logan, if we're going to have all these kids, the extra money I earn won't hurt, will it?"

He grinned. "I think I can safely say that the extra money won't hurt at all, my love. In fact, it'll be a pleasure not to worry about having to budget all the time."

They kissed, deeply, lingeringly. "I love you so much, Krista," Logan said huskily as he gazed into her soft blue eyes.

Krista was unbuttoning his shirt as he spoke. She removed his tie with one deft movement. He stilled her hand. "Darling, let me carry you upstairs."

"Not just yet." She slipped his suit coat from his shoulders and dropped it onto the floor. "First, I'm going to undress you right here in the hall. And then we're going to make love on the sofa. And *then* we'll proceed to the bedroom."

"I love a woman who takes charge," said Logan, and proceeded to demonstrate just how much.

Epilogue

"You're never going to believe who I received a letter from!" Logan said as he entered the bright pink and white nursery where Krista sat in the rocking chair nursing three-month-old Erica. He leaned down and kissed Krista's mouth lightly, then stroked his baby daughter's soft black curls. Erica paused to give him a toothless, liquid grin.

"An unbelievable letter, hmm?" Krista said, smiling at her husband. "It's from Mitch and he's written to tell us that he doesn't need money or a car?"

Logan laughed. "That *will* be the day!" Mitch was studying metallurgical engineering at Lehigh University and was leading an extremely active social life, although, thankfully, his grades were good. "No, honey, this is from Ned and Elaine Bolger. Remember them?"

Krista's eyes widened. "I remember. You sentenced them to a marriage counselor in hopes of a reconciliation. For months I kept expecting to read in the paper that one had murdered the other."

Logan arched his brows. "The Bolgers are fully reconciled and have renewed their marriage vows in a church ceremony. They wanted to thank me, even though it took them well over a year of counseling to

182

me to terms with each other. They heard from
oss Perry that we'd moved to Garrett County and
ked him for our address."

"I'm glad for the Bolgers. Although I find it hard to
elieve they're back together. That was one marriage
never thought could be saved."

"That's why I'm a judge and you're a lawyer,
veetheart."

She gave him a dry look. Little Erica finished
ursing, and Krista propped the baby over her shoul-
er and gently rubbed her small, warm back.

"There is a certain marriage that I don't think
ands a chance, though." Logan took the baby from
rista and cradled her in his big hands. "Mal Ches-
r stopped in to see me today. He wanted to know if
ou had time to handle his . . . er, divorce from Amy
ue."

"Uh-oh."

"He went against the advice of his lawyer at the
me of the wedding and didn't have a prenuptial
ontract drawn up."

"And Amy Sue is going to demand a settlement
at will set her up for life." Krista rolled her eyes.
ll have to think about taking on that one."

"Mal says he heard you're the best divorce lawyer
Garrett County," Logan said, his ebony eyes alight
ith pride. "I told him it was true."

The sound of footsteps scrambling up the stairs
ought the conversation to a halt. Lauren burst
to the room, her ponytail flying. The two cats were
her heels. "Mom, Dad, I'm home!" she announced
nnecessarily. She gave Krista and Logan each a
uick hug, then turned her attention to the baby
ho was beaming at her.

"Erica missed me," Lauren informed them hap-
ly. "Let me hold her, Daddy."

Logan handed her the baby and the two sisters
rinned at each other. Krista put her arm around
ogan's waist and leaned against him. She treasured

these quiet family moments—along with the row
dier, more boisterous family times, too. There wou
be good times and bad, but they were all in
together.

"I love you," Logan said quietly, his lips again
her ear.

"And I love you," she murmured back.

Again, footsteps sounded on the stairs. "Hi!" D
nise said as she joined them in the nursery. "Mom
have a favor to ask. You see, I want to go to th
dance on Friday with Tommy Johnson, but he hasn
asked me yet and I heard from Katie at school tod:
that Jeff Axton was going to ask me, so when th
phone rings, could you answer it and if it's Jeff te
him . . . uh . . . um . . ."

"You're incapacitated with a fever of one hundre
and six?" suggested Krista.

"You'll call him back as soon as you return fro:
Europe?" added Logan.

Denise stood between Logan and Krista and p
her arms around each one, laughing and huggir
them. "You two catch on fast."

THE EDITOR'S CORNER

I'm really impressed with the talent so many of you display for writing heart-wrenching letters! I get a lot of them about how long you have to wait for good reading between groups of LOVESWEPTs. For all of you who feel that way—and especially those of you who've written to me—I have a special FLASH bulletin. On sale right now is a fabulous novel that I believe you will want to read immediately. It's from Bantam (of course!) and is titled **WILD MIDNIGHT**. It's written by a wonderfully talented and versatile author named Maggie Davis. For a long time I've had a hunch that many women would enjoy as much as I a tale combining a number of elements: fiery sensuality, thoroughly up-to-date gothic elements in a completely believable context, and—most of all—primary characters one can really care about and root for. Trouble was, no one was writing such a book. Then along came Maggie Davis. **WILD MIDNIGHT** has thrills and chills, twists and turns galore, and a wonderfully torrid and touching romance between two unforgettable lovers. Grab a copy while you can!

As always, we're delighted to bring you a brand-new talent: Susan Richardson. Susan's first published novel is **FIDDLIN' FOOL**, LOVESWEPT #186. When an utterly charming Scottish rogue and accomplished fiddler, Jamie McLeod, performs in Sarah Hughes's hometown, he manages to turn her world upside down! His music is as wild, free, and utterly mesmerizing as the man himself. Sarah is captivated—but still part of her holds back, not believing the magic between her and Jamie could ever last. You'll be as enchanted as Sarah when Jamie sets out to woo her with thrilling music and sweet seduction.

A long time ago I read that Louisa May Alcott said that when she wrote she was "swept into a vortex" from which there was no escape (not even for sleeping or eating) until her tale was put on paper. Now, Iris

(continued)

Johansen tells me she doesn't write in the way that Ms. Alcott did, but the effect for the reader certainly is one of being "swept into a vortex." And nowhere is that storytelling power of Iris's more evident than in LOVESWEPT #187, **LAST BRIDGE HOME**. Elizabeth Ramsey is soon to give birth to the child of her late husband Mark, who was tragically killed in an auto accident during Elizabeth's first weeks of pregnancy. Then Jon Sandell, a stranger claiming to be Mark's best friend, moves into Elizabeth's life, ostensibly to protect her. But soon she realizes that her heart, her soul, belong to Jon and that the jeopardy he has told her she's in is very real indeed. This marvelous, complex love story—full of surprises—is one that I bet you'll never forget.

Again, it is a real delight for us to be able to introduce a new writer. Becky Lee Weyrich publishes her first contemporary romance novel with us. (You may have seen some of Becky's exciting long historical novels on bookracks in the last couple of years.) Becky debuts in **DETOUR TO EUPHORIA**, LOVESWEPT #188, a dilly of a book that's set in a small town in Georgia. From Sibyl Blanchard's arrest by the local sheriff to her near cardiac arrest over the charms of local lawyer Nick Fremont, who comes to bail her out, **DETOUR TO EUPHORIA** is a straight road into delightful romance. Nick brings Sibyl to his family's plantation house, and she feels as though she's stepped into a dream . . . until the time for her appearance in court draws near, and with it the end of her detour into Nick's arms. We predict you're going to grow very fond of each and every one of the wildly, wonderfully Southern (and infinitely believable) characters in this love story . . . and that you'll never forget a little Georgia town named Euphoria.

Be prepared to chuckle . . . and cheer . . . and be downright enchanted by Kay Hooper's **IN SERENA'S WEB**, LOVESWEPT #189! This is "vintage" Kay telling the story of Serena Jameson, who has the look of

(continued)

an angel, the sexiness of a true temptress, and the devilish determination of Satan himself. Why, Serena can be nothing short of ruthless when she makes up her mind to get something and there's a wee obstacle or two in the way! Poor Brian Ashford! You have to feel just a little bit sorry for the handsome industrialist as he gets drawn into our heroine's web. He even thinks *he's* protecting *her*—from playboy Joshua Long, among others. Then Serena gets a double-whammy she richly deserves, and you'll be right on the edge of your chair as danger and desire tangle the lives of these delightful people. Be sure to pay strict attention to that rakish Joshua, because Kay isn't through with him, not by a long shot! Am I teasing you mercilessly? Just in case I am, I'll give you a sneak preview: Stay tuned for **RAVEN ON THE WING,** LOVESWEPT #193, by Kay, coming next month.

Warm wishes,

Sincerely,

Carolyn Nichols

Carolyn Nichols
  Editor
LOVESWEPT
Bantam Books, Inc.
666 Fifth Avenue
New York, NY 10103